MIZO MYTHS

Second Edition

by

Cherrie Lalnunziri Chhangte

PUBLICATIONS
PRIVATE LIMITED

Blaft Publications Pvt. Ltd.
4/192 Ellaiamman Koil St.
Neelankarai
Chennai 600115
India
https://blaft.com

ISBN 978-93-80636-54-2

Cover illustration by Alyssa Pachuau

Table of Contents

Introduction

Nestled in a tiny little corner of the southernmost tip of Northeast India, the state of Mizoram is a land of contradictions. On the one hand, it is attuned to and influenced by the forces of modernization and westernization; since the late 1890s, when British missionaries introduced the written script and western education along with Christianity, Mizo society and culture have undergone a huge transformation. Yet, the state also retains its tribal roots and history. For all its embracement of modernity, it remains shrouded in legends and myths, the legacy of generations of Mizo people who sat basking in the warmth of the hearth, listening to stories of mythical times and heroic deeds.

As you begin these tales, be prepared to be transported into a world of lovely maidens and brave warriors; magical beings with the power to speak through dreams; and animals that can talk, sing, or compose poetry as the situation may demand. Especially fascinating, for me at least, are the romances between humans and supernatural creatures—weretigers, demons, sprites, fairies, and goblins—and the ease with which these fantastical couplings are narrated, as though they were perfectly natural occurrences.

My interest in Mizo folktales was awakened much after I had forayed into the world of literary studies. I realized that nearly all narratives can be traced back to folk stories. Tribal societies in general are very rich in oral narratives, and within these narratives the wisdom, beliefs, preoccupations, and folkways of a people can be discerned. At the core of seemingly simple tales are embedded folk attitudes regarding social structures, gender relations, spiritual beliefs and practices, relationships with nature, and survival strategies. Moreover, elements of song and dance, the poetic and the prosaic, the mythical and the ridiculous, all come together to form a unique fabric of narrative structures that are unlike any other "modern" plot—and yet paradoxically use the same archetypes found in so much of today's literature, in any genre.

In any translated work, it is inevitable that something of the original is lost. There are no equivalents for many Mizo words and phrases in the English language, simply because the meanings are inherently tied to the cultural contexts that have produced them. In a few cases, I have retained Mizo words in an attempt to stay as true to the original versions as possible. Some of the folktales contain poetry that is not in Duhlian (which in common usage is referred to as the "Mizo language"), but from related languages used by other tribes under the umbrella of Mizo: for example, in "The Story of Chawngtinleri," the lines that Chawngtinleri and her brother Liana call out to each other are in the Pawi language (also known as Lai).

Readers may also note that when a character is addressed, the last vowel of their name is dropped; thus Chawngtinleri calls her brother "Lian", and Liana calls his sister "Chawngtinler". It would sound very wrong to a Mizo reader to keep the final vowel!

Originality is another controversial area when it comes to oral narratives. The lack of written records makes it impossible to verify sources or arrive at universally accepted versions, since the telling of these stories is an activity necessarily coloured by personal interpretations and regional biases. I have attempted to translate the versions that seem to be most widely accepted, but there are, of course, many variations. An instance of regional differences is seen in the name of Khualtungamtawna, who is also known as Hualtungamtawna in some regions.

Since these stories were traditionally repeated over and over to many generations of children, certain elements recur in different tales. Two stories with very different beginnings can wind up with nearly identical endings. Readers familiar with English folktales or the Brothers Grimm will find familiar motifs in new combinations.

The stories in this collection are attempts not only to translate, but to transcreate what has been orally handed down over generations. There are a few places where I have added a detail or embellished the plot to make for easier reading; but for the most part, I have not veered far from the standard versions. The reader will note that the stories do not always follow the normal rules of cause-and-effect; logical linear progression is not in the nature of many folk narratives. It would be wise to take them simply as they are, without seeking realistic, logical, or rational explanations—especially given that most of these tales contain a liberal dose of magic.

Translation is often a tedious activity, demanding a fluent knowledge of at least two languages, and a thorough understanding of the cultural nuances that produce such narratives. I would like to thank my publishers, Rakesh Khanna and Blaft Publications, for taking on this enterprise with me. It has been a lengthy process to bring out even this small collection, with long absences abroad and the general business of life getting in the way. Rakesh has been a meticulous and well-informed editor, taking pains to research Mizo folktales and history, and always respectful of my wishes to stay as close to the sources as possible. I am also indebted to the various Mizo texts that I have used as sources and guides for my translations, notably the Serkawn Graded Readers by Nuchhungi, *Mizo Thawnthu* (various volumes) by Lalhmachhuana Zofa, and *Mizo Hnahthlak Thawnthu* (various volumes) by R.L. Thanmawia. For help with obscure terms and words, I am indebted to the *Dictionary of the Lushai Language* by J.H. Lorrain and Mizo scholar F. Lalzuithanga.

I hope you enjoy these stories.

—Cherrie Lalnunziri Chhangte

The Story of Tumchhingi & Raldawna

Long ago there lived a handsome young man named Raldawna. One day, when he was working with his mother to clear a jhum field, he happened upon a nightshade plant. The bright red berries of the plant struck him as very beautiful; in fact, he thought it was the most beautiful sight he had ever seen.

"Mother, do you think it's possible that there is a girl somewhere who is as beautiful as this fruit?" asked Raldawna.

"Certainly," said his mother. "Her name is Tumchhingi, and she lives in the valley below."

"Then let me go look for her," pleaded Raldawna. His mother gave him her permission, and taking the nightshade berry and his trusty slingshot with him, he set out to look for Tumchhingi.

Outside the first house he came to, Raldawna saw a young lady weaving on a loom. The fabric on the loom obscured her face. Raldawna took a small stone and shot it at the upper part of the cloth, causing it to flap away for a moment so he could have a glimpse of the girl. But she was not as beautiful as the nightshade fruit, so he walked onwards.

He came to a second house, and there, too, was a girl weaving on a loom. Again he shot a stone at her cloth with his slingshot, and again there was no comparison to the beauty of the fruit.

But finally, he came upon a house that he knew at once was Tumchhingi's. She was sitting on a large gong, weaving a puan on a loom, with a gun placed at her feet. She was exquisitely beautiful. The girl noticed him staring at her. "What are you looking for?" she asked.

Raldawna explained that he was searching for a girl as ruddy and beautiful as the nightshade fruit, and that now he had found her.

Tumchhingi replied, "If you want to marry me, you must first talk to my parents." So Raldawna went to meet her parents and asked for their permission to marry their daughter. They consented happily.

And so Raldawna and Tumchhingi were married. Tumchhingi gathered up all her possessions and left to follow her husband to his home.

After they had travelled a long way, Tumchhingi said, "Raldawn, I was sure I had packed all my belongings. But I just realized that I've forgotten my bronze comb."

"All right," he replied, "I'll leave you here on this banyan tree while I go back for your comb." He lifted Tumchhingi up and sat her down in a safe spot in the branches of the tree, and then headed back the way they had come.

Not long afterwards, a Phungpuinu happened by. (A Phungpuinu is an extremely ugly sort of goblin. They are always female, and usually not very nice.) The Phungpuinu was walking along muttering to herself and trampling on cucumber peel, and she passed right under Tumchhingi's tree.

As she passed below the spot where Tumchhingi was sitting, the Phungpuinu caught sight of Tumchhingi's shadow on the ground. The Phungpuinu mistook it for her own shadow, and she stopped to admire her beautiful figure. Then she sang a little song:

"I myself wear no ornaments, but look!
My shadow wears bangles, jingle jangle,
My shadow wears necklaces, jingle jangle."

The Phungpuinu swayed back and forth as she sang these words standing beneath the tree. Tumchhingi sat on her perch looking down at her. She knew it would be better to hold her tongue, but after watching the Phungpuinu swaying for some time, she was so annoyed she could not help herself. "Phungpuinu, that is not your shadow," she called out. "It's mine."

The Phungpuinu looked up, saw Tumchhingi, and scowled at her. "Oh! And how did you climb up there, Tumchhing?" she asked.

Tumchhingi replied, "I climbed up on my back."

The Phungpuinu stood with her back to the tree and tried to shimmy up, but she did not get very far before she fell with a hard thump.

"Tell me seriously, how did you climb up there, Tumchhing?" she asked again.

Tumchhingi replied, "I climbed up sideways."

The Phungpuinu stood with her side to the tree, and tried to climb up sideways, but again she fell with a thump. She asked a third time, "How did you climb up there, Tumchhing?" and this time, Tumchhingi told her the truth. The Phungpuinu then climbed right up to where Tumchhingi was sitting.

"Will you look for lice in my hair?" the Phungpuinu asked Tumchhingi, and sat down in front of her on the branch, with her back to her. Trembling with fright, Tumchhingi began to comb her fingers through the goblin's wild, bushy hair. Soon she found head lice so fat they were the size of small brinjals.

"Now you must crunch them up!" said the Phungpuinu. Tumchhingi pretended to eat the lice, but really she threw them to the ground.

Then it was the Phungpuinu's turn. They switched places, and the Phungpuinu began to examine Tumchhingi's head. But she could not find a single louse. Looking at Tumchhingi's clean, white scalp, the greedy Phungpuinu began to get hungry.

"Let me wear your puan for a while," she said to the girl. Trembling with fright, Tumchhingi took off her puan and gave it to her.

"Let me wear your blouse for a while," she asked next, and Tumchhingi gave it to her.

"Let me wear your bangles and your necklaces," she asked next, and Tumchhingi gave those to her too, and now the Phungpuinu was dressed in everything Tumchhingi had been wearing.

Then the Phungpuinu opened her mouth very wide and swallowed the girl in one gulp!

After a long while, Raldawna returned to the tree, and it seemed to him that Tumchhingi looked very different. "Tumchhing, why is it that your eyes look so stretched?" he asked.

"I kept straining them, looking in the distance, waiting to see you return. That is why they are stretched," she replied.

"And why is it that your fingers are so long and pointy, like talons?" asked Raldawna.

"From the moment you left, I kept pointing in the direction you went. That is why they have become long and pointy," she replied.

And so Raldawna took the Phungpuinu home.

The people in his village knew about his marriage, and they were all waiting for his return. "Raldawna is bringing home the beautiful Tumchhingi!" they told each other, as they swept the pathways and spread out their puan on the ground. But then they saw Raldawna walking into the village with the Phungpuinu, and they all exclaimed, "Oh no! I won't let that Phungpuinu walk on my puan!" Hurriedly, they all took away their puan, so that Raldawna had to walk on a bare path as he took his new bride into his home.

A few days later, while Raldawna was out in the jhum field, the Phungpuinu went to the outskirts of the village and vomited violently. She brought up what was left of Tumchhingi, which was just a tiny seed. Soon the seed germinated, and before many days had passed it grew into a large bottle-gourd vine. But the plant only bore a single fruit, which grew very high up on the vine, higher than any passer-by could reach.

Eventually Raldawna came that way, and he managed to pluck the gourd. He took it home and dried it and kept it for storing seeds.

Unbeknownst to Raldawna, Tumchhingi still lived inside the gourd. Whenever the house was empty, she would come out and cook food for her husband and his family, and then go back inside the gourd to hide from the Phungpuinu.

Raldawna was very perplexed as to who was preparing food for them every day in his absence, and he was determined to solve the mystery. One morning, he left to the jhum fields along with his family, but then quickly turned back and waited outside the house to see who would cook the food. When Tumchhingi came out of the gourd and started cooking, Raldawna ran and caught her in his arms, overjoyed.

"No, let me go! I must go back inside the gourd, or the Phungpuinu will swallow me again," said Tumchhingi. But Raldawna would not let her go.

Just then the Phungpuinu came back, carrying a basket of arum stalks to feed the pigs. She laid the basket down outside and tried to come in, but Raldawna would not open the door. Angrily, the Phungpuinu broke down the door and stormed in. When she saw Tumchhingi she became even more furious, and threatened to kill her.

"Wait. We will have a competition between the two of you," said Raldawna. Then he brought two daos. To the Phungpuinu he gave a very blunt dao, but to his wife he gave a very sharp dao. He also gave the Phungpuinu an ordinary cloth to wear as armour, but to his wife he gave a thick blanket.

The Phungpuinu struck Tumchhingi first, but the blow caused her no harm. Then it was Tumchhingi's turn, and with one slash of her sharp dao she cut the Phungpuinu in two.

Tumchhingi and Raldawna threw out the two halves of the Phungpuinu's dead body. And then they lived happily ever after.

The Story of Khualtungamtawna & the Weretigers

Once upon a time there was a man called Khualtungamtawna. He was famed as a great hunter, and the walls of his hut were covered with trophies—the skulls of all the animals he had brought down with his arrows. Every day, he and his faithful dog would go into the forest, looking for more wild animals to hunt. Sometimes, however, he would feel a little lonely, and think to himself, "What good is it being such a successful hunter when I have no one to share my success with?" For Khualtungamtawna was not married yet; he lived all alone with his daughter, Chemteii (whose mother he had never married), and his dog.

One day, Khualtungamtawna set off to hunt in a place where he had once been fortunate enough to shoot a tumpang, a type of wild buffalo that was considered a lucky catch for hunters. This was an area that was rumoured to be populated by tigers; but Khualtungamtawna was a brave man, and he often went hunting there anyway.

That day, as he walked through the dense forest, he did indeed happen upon a tiger. Khualtungamtawna had his bow and arrow at the ready, and with the stealthy moves of a seasoned hunter, he crouched down low, determined to make his move before the beast saw him. Silently, carefully, he took aim, and released his arrow. His shot was true, and he felled the animal before it even knew he was there. Standing over his victim, Khualtungamtawna chanted exultantly:

"Hear me! My fame will never fade,
For I have felled the striped tiger in his tracks!"

He then proceeded home, leaving the tiger carcass behind for his friends to collect later. The news spread quickly, and the entire village was soon abuzz with excited chatter about Khualtungamtawna's latest feat. The villagers were all in awe of this greatest of hunters, and they proudly recounted stories of all the other times this brave man had encountered tigers near the village, and how he had always emerged unscathed, and how he always managed to kill the ferocious beasts in the end.

A few days later, Khualtungamtawna called his daughter Chemteii and said to her, "My daughter, I am going away for a few days to look for a bride in one of the neighboring villages. You stay at home and take good care of the house, and I shall be back soon."

Chemteii replied, "Yes, father, I will stay at home and take care of everything. But I will miss you and our dog very much."

In the village next to theirs was the village of the Keimi, or Weretigers. The chief of the village himself was a Weretiger (though not all the inhabitants were so), and he was furious with Khualtungamtawna for having killed so many of his brothers. For a long time, the Keimi had been plotting how best to avenge the deaths of the Keimi at the hands of Khualtungamtawna.

The chief of the Keimi village had a beautiful daughter named Keimingi, who also had two handsome and gallant brothers. Keimingi had often wondered about Khuatungamtawna: what kind of a person was this, who had killed so many of her relatives?

When the weretiger men heard the latest news, that yet another one of their cousins had been struck down by Khualtungamtawna, they began discussing how to get back at him. In the house of the chief, especially, the talk always revolved around their nemesis and his skills as a hunter.

"Be wary of Khualtungamtawna," the chief would caution his remaining sons. "He kills whoever he comes across."

But his sons would reply with bravado, "We are not afraid of him! We can take him on!"

When she heard them talk this way, their sister Keimingi only became more and more curious about this man who had brought so much danger and fear into their lives.

Meanwhile, Khualtungamtawna, who had been travelling and roaming the countryside with no set destination in mind, one day came across the Keimi village. Standing on a hilltop overlooking the village, he surveyed the activities of the villagers. "It looks like an interesting place," he thought. "I will pay it a visit." As he approached the village, he was impressed by the clean and well-kept paths that led to it. "What a good chief and elders they must have, to maintain this place so well!" he thought.

Upon entering the village, the first person he happened to see was a beautiful maiden chopping wood. As he glanced around, the whole village seemed to be busy with various chores. He stood there taking in the scene, trying to determine where he would ask for a place to stay—while also surreptitiously feasting his eyes on the beautiful maiden, absorbed in her task of chopping wood. As he went nearer, he thought, "She is beautiful enough from afar… but up close, she is truly breathtaking!" The maiden had become aware of his intense stare, though she showed no outward sign of having noticed him. "How this stranger stares at me!" she thought to herself. "He is so ruddy and handsome!" Khualtungamtawna, for his part, felt a rush of emotions—this woman was so beautiful that he felt he had been wasting his life until this moment, not having met her until now. He longed to tell her how much he desired her. Even if she didn't feel the same way for him, he felt he owed it to her to tell her!

Meanwhile, the girl, distracted by his presence, was having trouble chopping her big log. No matter how hard she swung her axe, she could not split it. As Khualtungamtawna continued to stare at her, she became all the more embarrassed.

Eventually, he moved on, determined to find a host as soon as possible so that he could have a bath, freshen up, and call upon her again before any of the village lads could beat him to it. Soon some people greeted him, asking his name and where he was from, and after introducing himself he arranged to stay at their house.

As soon as he had a chance, Khualtungamtawna asked his hostess about the maiden he had seen earlier.

"Oh, she is Keimingi, the daughter of our chief," his hostess replied. "We are very proud of her." After gathering this bit of information, Khualtungamtawna set out for the chief's house to pay a visit to the woman of his dreams.

Seeing her still at work in the courtyard, he approached her and introduced himself. She replied, "So you are the famed hunter, Khualtungamtawna! I have heard your name." He then offered to help her with her wood cutting, and despite her protests, he took the axe from her. Muscles rippling, he raised the axe high above his head and brought it down with full force, splitting the log in half with a single stroke. Keimingi was very impressed.

"Not only is he handsome, he's strong as well," she mused. "Just the kind of man I want." Once the work was done, they proceeded inside, so that she could offer him a cup of tea, as is customary when a man goes calling on a woman. Khualtungamtawna was smitten; he could think of nothing except how beautiful and kind she was, and how he had already fallen head over heels in love with her.

Inside the house, they sat and talked, and lost no time in telling each other how they felt. Khualtungamtawna said that if she felt the same way about him as he did about her, then he wanted to send emissaries immediately to arrange for their marriage. Keimingi assured him that she had no objections, but that he should meet her parents, the chief and his wife, so that they could give their consent first.

Khualtungamtawna went back to his hosts, and when he related these events to them over dinner, they were encouraging. They told him that he and Keimingi would make a perfect match; none of the men in the village had dared to woo her yet, though she was already of marriageable age. That night, Khualtungamtawna, like a man who has found a valuable treasure and refuses to let go of it, headed off once more to Keimingi's house, and once again he pressed the issue of marriage. She replied demurely that women had very little say in the matter, and it was a decision for her parents to make.

The next morning, at the urging of his guest, Khualtungamtawna's host set out for his chief's house. He went as an emissary, to ask for Keimingi's hand in marriage. He entered the chief's house and made his request directly, that the chief's daughter be allowed to marry his guest, the famed hunter Khualtungamtawna. Keimingi's parents, realizing that here was a golden opportunity to take revenge upon their dreaded enemy, made no objection to the alliance.

Khualtungamtawna's host went back to his house and told Khualtungamtawna, who had been waiting nervously, what the chief's family had said: that Khualtungamtawna would be married to their daughter on any day that he chose, and could take her home to his village at any time thereafter. Khualtungamtawna was overjoyed to hear the good news.

Soon, the village witnessed the marriage of the two lovers, and the day soon came when it was time to leave for Khualtungamtawna's home. Keimingi's family came to the edge of the village to see her off, and she bid them a fond farewell.

As they approached Khualtungamtawna's village, they were welcomed by wellwishers at the outskirts, each one eager for a glimpse of the blushing bride—who, everyone agreed, was exceptionally beautiful. Soon the newlyweds reached Khualtungamtawna's hut. As the groom excitedly led his bride inside, Keimingi exclaimed in surprise: for the walls were adorned with the heads of all kinds of animals. Though she had known before that Khualtungamtawna had killed many Keimi, she was filled with horror when she realized that among the other trophies on the walls were tiger skulls that had been the heads of her own brothers. Still, she had the presence of mind not to show any outward reaction, and proceeded to do all the little chores that needed attention in the house, and to perform her duties as hostess to the many friends who dropped in to offer their congratulations. Once alone, though, she would stare at the trophies mounted on the walls of the hut, weeping for her dead relations and dabbing at her eyes. How could her brothers, who had been so brave and magnificent in life, now be reduced to mere ornaments on a wall? The more she thought about it, the more she was filled with seething hatred for her husband, and she soon was consumed by the need to avenge her brothers' deaths.

As time passed, the newlywed couple settled into domestic life. On the surface, all seemed well. But Keimingi, constantly reminded of her family's loss, could not get over her anger. She was unhappy, and obsessed about the best way to take revenge. Khualtungamtawna knew of his wife's nature, and he was secretly aware of how she felt, but he did not know how to address the issue. Little rifts began to appear in their relationship, but neither was willing to talk about it. And so life went on.

One day, Keimingi and her stepdaughter Chemteii went into the forest to gather firewood. As they finished their work, Keimingi spotted a lone deer that seemed like easy prey. She asked Chemteii to go on home without her, saying that since she wanted to go into a thicker part of the forest to answer the call of nature. The young girl agreed; but she had a suspicion that her stepmother was up to something, so she followed her at a distance. Keimingi, unaware that she was being shadowed, went deep into the undergrowth until she was sure nobody could see her, and then turned herself into a tiger.

Chemteii stood transfixed, gazing in horror, as she watched her stepmother transform before her very eyes, and begin circling her prey, crouched low and ready to pounce. As she circled, Keimingi caught sight of her stepdaughter standing there watching her, but she was so focused on stalking her victim that she was no longer bothered about the possibility of being discovered. Chemteii rushed home, fleeing for dear life, afraid that she herself would become her stepmother's next quarry. She ran home into her father's arms, and after much prompting, she sobbed out the entire story.

Later, father and daughter went to meet Keimingi, and were careful not to show any sign of distress. At dinner time, Khualtungamtawna asked his wife, "Did you do something to frighten Chemteii today, when you went into the woods?"

"Of course not," Keimingi replied casually.

Chemteii was terrified of her stepmother by this time, and she asked her father to end the marriage, but he refused. He pretended not to know what had happened. It was impossible now for Chemteii to feel relaxed when her stepmother was around; she was constantly filled with trepidation. Keimingi would threaten her and say, "You must be a good girl and obey me. You must tell no one what you saw.'" As a result of living in constant fear, Chemteii often fell sick and had to stay bedridden. Khualtungamtawna was aware of the reasons for her illness, but he loved Keimingi so much that he refused to consider divorcing her.

Time passed. One day, Khualtungamtawna decided to invite his in-laws home for a feast, for which he planned to slaughter a fattened pig. He sent a messenger to the Keimi village to extend an invitation on his behalf. The invitation was accepted with enthusiasm, and Keimingi's two brothers decided to attend the feast as well.

As they were about to leave the village, an old woman warned them to be careful, reminding them that Khualtungamtawna was famed as a hunter and had killed many of their brothers. Nevertheless, the young men set off towards their sister's village full of youthful exuberance. As soon as they had left their village and were in the thick of the jungle, they transformed themselves into tigers, roaring out their joy and excitement. When they reached the outskirts of their host's village, they concealed their true selves and took on human forms again. In high spirits, they reached their brother-in-law's hut where they were given a warm welcome. However, their mood was quickly dampened when they saw the dried skulls of their brothers proudly displayed on the walls. Like their sister before them, their thoughts at once turned to revenge.

At night, as Keimingi was preparing her brothers' bedding, they began to express their disgust and resentment of the way their brothers' skulls were displayed so brazenly on the walls. Keimingi shared her frustration and anger as well.

The household settled into sleep and the night grew quiet. The stillness of the night, however, was disturbed when the brothers got up and again started lamenting over the heads of their dead brothers, weeping brokenheartedly. They vowed revenge upon Khualtungamtawna, their killer. Chemteii was woken by the sounds of their crying and became very scared. She was afraid that these men had come to kill her father. Not knowing what else to do, she woke her father, asking him to take her outside so that she could pass urine. Her father sleepily objected, but finally gave in. Their guests appeared to be sleeping peacefully, which surprised Chemteii, since she had heard them crying just a few moments before. Once outside, Chemteii related what she had heard, and how the men had vowed to avenge the death of their brothers. Khualtungamtawna pondered over this, but assured his daughter that no harm would come to him.

When they went back inside after having finished their ablutions, they kindled the fire and sat together near it, pretending that there were rats about, and shooting arrows at them. Their guests could do nothing except pretend to sleep, and thus father and daughter remained unharmed.

The next morning, Khualtungamtawna woke his guests and asked them to drive the pig out from the pen below the house for slaughter. They saw this as a wonderful opportunity to kill both the pig and its owner, and they grinned at each other. Keimingi noticed her brothers' excitement, and she knew something was about to happen. As the brothers went underneath the house to drive out the pig, they turned themselves into tigers, planning to terrorize and kill their host too. They said to each other, "Let us pounce on him now; we may not have another chance."

But Khualtungamtawna was well prepared. As soon as they turned into menacing tigers and bared their teeth at him, he was ready with his bow and arrow. Before they had a chance to attack him, he shot and killed them both.

Keimingi shrieked in horror, but it was too late to warn them. She was consumed with fury. All she could think of was how to kill her husband and avenge her brothers. She wept bitterly, cradling her brothers' heads in her lap and threatening her husband with the fate that awaited him. Khualtungamtawna in vain tried to explain how he had acted in self-defense, but she would no longer listen. The fight became bitter, with Khualtungamtawna saying "They were trying to attack me!" and Keimingi responding "No, you always planned on killing them! They meant to kill the pig, not you! You've never really loved me!" and so on.

As this state of affairs continued, Khualtungamtawna desperately tried to make amends. Keimingi was with child now, and he was painfully aware that his wife wished him harm, so he became very careful. Even though he knew his wife was looking for an opportunity to kill him, he still loved her and was willing to do anything for her. He said to his wife, "Keiming, if it will please you, I will give you anything you want. Would you like to have some honey?" And Keimingi replied, "Yes, but if you are going to get some for me, get the stuff from the hive on the cliff." Khualtungamtawna trudged along, aware of the dangers of climbing the steep cliff to get the beehive, but willing to take the risk to placate his irate wife. He came back covered with bee stings, thanking his luck that he was not allergic to them. His wife, though, was disappointed that he had not been killed.

Keimingi kept thinking of other ways to get rid of him. One day, she said, "I feel like having some fresh meat. Why don't you go hunting? They say there's a herd of big boar over by that same cliff where the beehive was." She hoped he would fall off the cliff, or meet with some other accident. Khualtungamtawna was aware of his wife's intentions, but went anyway, taking his dog with him. Luck favoured him again, and once more, he came home with his kill, unharmed. That night, as he sat wondering what task his wife would set for him next, she came to him and said, "I'm in the mood to eat the meat of some wild boar, like the ones that are found to the north. The beast should have magnificent tusks, as long as the polished beam of a weaving loom."

So, when morning came, he once again set out with his dog to hunt for wild boar. They walked all day, for the place up north that his wife had mentioned was quite far away. Finally, he came to the edge of a cliff and surveyed the wilderness below him, where the wild boars roamed.

Next, Khualtungamtawna enchanted all the trees of the forest so that they would yield to his commands, and then he whistled to call out to the boars. He notched an arrow in his bow and waited for the boars to appear. The moment they did, he started shooting at them. With the trees of the forest under his enchantment, he could leap and soar across them with ease, staying well above the animals and out of harm's way. There were many boars that day, and although he felled every single one that appeared, they seemed to be an endless horde advancing towards him, and he became a little worried since he had jumped into their midst. But the trees helped him by moving according to his wishes, and every time an animal made a lunge for him, he would leap onto a tree and escape to safety.

When he had killed nearly all of the boars, the last one appeared before him. This was the most powerful of them all, with a magnificent tusk as long and lustrous as the polished beam of a weaving loom. Khualtungamtawna took aim and started shooting arrows at it, but the animal was adept at using its tusk to deflect most of the arrows. Even when an arrow did hit it, the beast would neither fall nor surrender. The huntsman became worried, but still he kept up his attack. Whenever the beast charged him, he leapt onto a nearby tree.

But when Khualtungamtawna had enchanted the trees of the forest, there was one that he had missed: the Phuanberh tree. When the boar charged at him again, Khualtungamtawna tried to leap onto the Phuanberh tree, but the tree would not hold him; the branch snapped off and he fell to the ground. The boar's attack mortally injured him. He lay prone, unable to move, dying.

Once the boar had gone, Khualtungamtawna's dog approached his master, wary, fearful, and helpless. Khualtungamtawna spoke to his faithful companion: "Go and run to the village and alert the people as to what has happened. They will come and try to carry my body on a stretcher made from tree branches, but they won't be able to do it. They must use woven sungrass. Then they will try to carry my body into my hut through the door, but they won't be able to do it. They must take me in through your entrance, the one under the door. When we get home, make sure you sit on the broom. When the mourners have departed, your mistress will want to sweep the house; she'll order you to move and try to kick you off the broom. When she does that, you must bite through the tendons in her leg behind the knee. In this way you must avenge me." As soon he heard his master's words, the dog rushed off to do his bidding.

When Khualtungamtawna's dog reached the village, people noticed that it had come home without his master, and that it was acting strangely, They decided that something must be wrong, and followed it back into the forest where he led them to the place where his master lay. By the time they got there, he was no longer breathing. They proceeded to make arrangements to carry him, but just as Khualtungamtawna had predicted, they were unable to carry him on a stretcher made from tree branches. The branches kept breaking when they placed his body on them. The dog brought over some sungrass; realizing what it wanted them to do, they began to collect more sungrass and weave the strands together. In this way they were able to carry Khualtungamtawna's body home. But when they got there, they found they were unable to carry him inside the house through the door. The dog yelped and whimpered, going in and out of its own entrance under the doorway. Finally, they understood what the dog was trying to convey, and they brought the body under the doorway through the dog's entrance. In this way they were able to bring him inside the house.

Keimingi made a show of weeping copiously over her husband's dead body, but secretly she felt happy and relieved that revenge had at last been carried out. Later, when most of the mourners had left, she tried to sweep the house, but the dog refused to budge from its seat on top of the broom. Exasperated, she said, "Get out of the way, you cur!" and kicked it. But as she did this, the dog bit her as hard as it could at the spot where its master had told it to, and then it ran away. As a result of this attack Keimingi became incapacitated, and she could not enjoy the rest of her days. She died not long after, having become infirm and disabled.

As he had expressed his wish before, Khualtungamtawna was buried in the spot of his choosing, near the Hnahkiah tree, a tree which bears large leaves and clusters of small lavender-colored flowers. Some say that Khualtungamtawna's "dog" was in fact a wolf, and that after his death, this wolf used to carry the heart and liver of whatever animal it killed and place them at the grave of its master. It is said that to this day, when a wolf makes a kill, it will leave the heart and liver near a Hnahkiah tree.

The Story of Rimenhawihi

Rimenhawihi was a beautiful woman. She had a husband whose name was Zawlthlia and they were deeply in love with each other. Rimenhawihi was famed far and wide for her beauty. She was especially known for her long, beautiful tresses. She was well aware of the beauty of her lustrous locks, and would often admire herself. There was a river near her home, and Rimenhawihi would go there to bathe and wash her hair.

Once, when she was bathing in this river, a single strand of her long hair fell from her head and into the river. There, the strand of hair was swallowed by a fish, and because it was so long, it made the fish feel very full indeed.

Now, there was a chief in a village towards the foot of the river. One day, he called his servants and ordered them to catch some fish for his meal. His servants happened to catch the very fish that had swallowed the strand of Rimenhawihi's hair. It was a big fish with a protruding belly. Curious, the men cut open its belly and found it full of hair. As they unraveled it, they found to their amazement that it was just a single strand. It was such an unusual sight to see that they decided to bring it home to their master.

When the chief of the village saw the exceptionally long strand of hair they had found inside the fish's belly, he was astonished. He immediately dispatched his men to locate the owner of the hair.

He sent them towards the mouth of the river, guessing that it must have come from there.

The men followed the path of the river upstream and finally reached Rimenhawihi's house. Her house was made of iron, and when they attempted to go in, they could not do so, for she had barricaded herself inside for safety since her husband Zawlthlia was away. Since they could not enter her house, the men stood outside and sang to her:

"You in the house of iron,
You in the house of brass,
Reveal to us your name."

She sang back:

"I have no name, no name,
I am She-Who-Lives-On-Water,
I am She-Who-Lives-On-Boiled-Leaves."

After this exchange, the men left her house and went home to their chief and told him what had transpired. However, he said, "Nobody is named those names. Go back and find out her real name!" and so they went back once more.

When they reached her house, the men once again asked her to reveal her name, and once more, she replied in the same way. When the men went back to convey this to their chief, he was not satisfied. He kept sending them back again and again. Finally, when they had asked her many times to reveal her name, she relented and told them:

"I am Rimenhawihi,
Also known as Menchanghawihi."

When she finally told them her name, they were very excited and rushed home to tell the chief. They were so afraid of forgetting her name that they kept repeating "Men, men, men" on the way home; even when they happened to stumble upon anything on the road, they exclaimed, "Men!"

When they finally reached the chief's house, alas! there was nobody who could remember her full name. At last, they told the chief, "She says her name is Men." This angered the chief, for he knew a maiden would not simply have the name "Men". He said tersely, "Go back right away, and if you dare to return without knowing her full name, you shall see what will happen to you!"

So the men once more hurried back to Rimenhawihi's house, and as usual, they stood outside her house and asked her the same question once more, and she gave them the same reply as before. This time, however, the men were able to remember, and they went back and told the chief her true, full name. The chief, finally satisfied with their information, paced around mulling over what he had heard, and then proclaimed to his men, "Well, now that we know her true, full name, whether she has a partner or not, bring her to me!"

Once again, the men went back to Rimenhawihi's house as they were bid by their master. Her husband Zawlthlia was away hunting for the night, and he had again locked his beautiful wife inside for fear of anyone trying to steal her while he was away. The chief's men tried to enter the house from all sides but to no avail. Eventually they decided to climb up on the roof; from there, they threw down the various fruits the chief had sent with them as gifts for Rimenhawihi to entice her. Rimenhawihi ignored their gestures for quite a while, until they dropped their choicest fruits—oranges—down into her house.

When she saw the oranges, Rimenhawihi could no longer contain herself, and reached out to take one. As she came within their reach, one of the men managed to grab a lock of her hair. When she realized the man had hold of her hair, Rimenhawihi, proud and possessive of her beautiful tresses, allowed herself to be captured rather than struggle and risk having it pulled out.

Rimenhawihi, however, was a clever girl. Once she was captured by the men, she quickly and slyly told all the domestic animals in her house—the dog, the chickens—that she had been forced to go with her captors and that she would keep leaving strands of her hair as clues along the way, and to convey this urgently to her husband as soon as he came home. Then she left with the men.

After some time, her husband, who had spent the night in the forest, came home. As soon as they saw him, the dog and chickens gathered around him in agitation. He first asked the dog: "Dog, where is your mistress?"

"Bauh, bauh, bauh,
She is over the horizon,
Follow the strands of hair."

Then he asked the chickens, who replied:

"Ti ti ik ik,
She is over the horizon,
Follow the strands of hair."

Quickly, without a moment's delay, Zawlthlia did as he was bid and started to follow their tracks. As he went further, he saw that there were strands of hair strewn along the way, and he followed them. After he had followed the direction of the strands for a long time, it started to get dark. When night fell, he finally caught up with his beloved wife and her captors. He killed all of the men who had kidnapped Rimenhawihi, and together they went home in the night.

For the rest of their lives, nobody tried to come between them again.

The Story of Nucchimi

Nuchhimi was a young girl who was travelling to her aunt's house along with her younger sister. As her parents sent her off with a packet of pork, they warned her that when she came to a fork in the road, she should take the neat and clean path which led to her aunt's house, not the dirty and messy one which led to Hmuichukchuriduninu's house.

Now, Hmuichukchuriduninu was an evil old woman who lived in the woods. She had a very long neck, and instead of a nose and mouth, she had a hard protruding beak, like a bird's.

Unbeknownst to Nucchimi and her parents, Hmuichukchuriduninu was hiding behind a nearby tree, and overheard their whole conversation. She quickly ran back and cleaned the path to her house, transferring all the dirt and rubbish to the other road.

So it was that when Nuchhimi and her sister came to the fork, they turned down the wrong path.

Hmuichukchuriduninu stood outside her house—a traditional bamboo structure on a raised platform—and welcomed the two girls, pretending to be their aunt. Nuchhimi was surprised by the woman's strange beak, but Hmuichukchuriduninu spoke kindly to them, saying "Welcome, dear girls! You must be tired after your journey; rest yourselves!" and served them a tasty meal. Soon Nuchhimi cast her suspicions aside.

As the sun set, Hmuichukchuriduninu told Nuchhimi to sleep in the corner, while she cradled the younger sister in her arms.

Late in the night, Hmuichukchuriduninu started pecking the girl's head with her beak, trying to crack her skull. The little girl cried out "Ka U! Big sister!" in pain. Nuchhimi was awakened by her sister's cries; but Hmuichukchuriduninu reassured her, saying that the girl was only crying because of insect bites. So Nuchhimi went back to sleep.

Meanwhile, the witch proceeded to kill the sister, eat her brain, drink her blood, devour her flesh, and throw her bones into the fireplace.

The next morning, Nuchhimi awoke to the grating voice of Hmuichukchuriduninu ordering her to prepare the fire for the morning meal. She went to make the fire, and there she discovered her sister's bones. She realised what had happened and began weeping.

Hmuichukchuriduninu impatiently said, "What is wrong with you? What makes you cry so piteously? Hurry up and make the fire." Nuchhimi, thinking it was best not to anger her, pretended that it was just the smoke from the fire making her eyes water.

After the morning meal, Hmuichukchuriduninu caught Nuchhimi, bound her hands and feet, put in her a basket, and tied the basket to the roof beams. Using her supernatural powers, she locked the house from both the inside and the outside, latching both sides of the door with wooden planks. Then she left to work in her jhum field, planning to eat the girl for supper that evening.

After she had gone, Nuchhimi heard a mouse scuttling about in the house. The mouse, moving around above her, made dust fall upon her. She whispered to the mouse, "Mr. Mouse, instead of making dust fall all over me, why don't you bite through the ropes holding up this basket I am trapped in?" The mouse did so; it also bit through the ropes that bound her. As soon as she was released, Nuchhimi thanked the mouse profusely, somehow managed to open the door, and ran home.

Her parents, horrified at her ordeal and enraged at the loss of their younger daughter, began to plan their revenge on Hmuichukchuriduninu.

While the old witch was out, they went to her house and prepared a complicated trap for her. First, they hid an egg inside the hearth. Then they put a snake in her water gourd. Next, they placed a nest of termites in her blanket. Next, they smeared night soil all over her bedpost. Next, they hid sharpened slivers of bamboo all across the thatched walls of the house. Next, they placed a large number of tiny biting red ants in the bamboo container where she kept her oil . Next, they left a huge wooden pestle at the other door of the hut. Finally, they left a ferocious dog, an angry goat, a wild boar, and a bull gayal in the space under the hut.

They said to the mouse, who was still there, "You must pretend to be Nuchhimi. If Hmuichukchuriduni calls for Nuchhimi, you must respond as if you were her." Then they left.

While Hmuichukchuriduninu was out in the field, she had caught a pregnant barking deer which she planned to slaughter. As she was carrying this animal home, she got caught in a torrential downpour, which left her sopping wet. As she got home, flustered and with her arms full, shaking with cold from being drenched in the rain, she shouted, "Ssss… sssss… sssss… Nuchhimi, open the door."

"I can't," answered the mouse. "You tied me up and hung me from the crossbeams, remember?"

Cursing, Hmuichukchuriduninu broke down the door in a rage. The mouse quickly hid inside a hollow bamboo.

When the old witch realised that Nuchhimi was gone, she became even angrier. Dripping wet and grumbling, she sat down by the hearth and lit a fire, still shivering, "Ssss… ssss… ssss." Almost as soon as the fire got going, the hot egg burst and splattered in her eye. She rushed to her water jug, but the snake leapt out of it and bit her on the face.

"Awi, awi, awi!" she screamed. "I'm in such pain! I'm going to crawl under my blanket and rest."

But as soon as she drew the blanket over herself, the termites crawled all over her and started biting her. She grabbed hold of the bedpost to try and pull herself out of bed, only to discover that it was covered with excrement. She tried to clean her hands by wiping them on the wall, but ended up shredding her flesh on the sharp edges of the bamboo slivers. Then she tried to pour oil on her wounds, but along with the oil came hundreds of red ants which bit her all over.

"This house is full of pests!" she shouted. "I have to get out!" She tried to run out the other door, but she banged right into the wooden pestle.

She stood on the platform at the front of her house, despondent. She realized that she had not only lost Nuchhimi; the barking deer had run away as well. "I've lost Nuchhimi, I've lost my deer!" she cried.

In a tantrum of agony and frustration, she began stomping up and down. Soon she broke through the platform and fell into the space underneath, where the ferocious dog, angry goat, wild boar, and enraged bull gayal set upon her and quickly tore her to pieces.

Nuchhimi and her parents went home and lived happily ever after.

The Story of Kungawrhi

Once upon a time, there was a man, a chief of a village, who was working in the forest, gathering materials to weave a basket. As he was splitting bamboo into thin strips for his basket, he accidentally cut his thumb with his sharp knife. Afterwards his thumb became infected. An abscess started to form, filled with pus. After a few days, the skin on the festering, swollen wound looked ready to break, so the man and his wife decided to make an incision and drain it. As the wound started to ooze, they discovered, to their immense surprise, a tiny baby that emerged along with the pus. It became clear that the swelling of the thumb meant that the thumb had not only been infected, it had actually been pregnant.

The little baby was a girl, and they named her Kungawrhi. At first, they fed the tiny baby just half a grain of millet. As she grew a little bigger, they would give her a bigger piece of millet, and then a whole grain of millet for each meal. They continued to nourish her, giving her more and more food as her appetite grew with her body.

As time went by, Kungawrhi grew healthier and stronger, until one day she was a fully grown, beautiful young lady. In the evenings, in the streets, she and her friends would play their favourite game: Inkawi Bah, which is played with big, dried beans of the Kawi plant. Players are divided into two teams. The dried beans are delicately placed upright on the ground, one bean for each player.

About six feet away from this line of beans, a line is drawn in the dirt, indicating the starting point for the opposing team. One by one, each team member takes their own favourite bean, often shiny and smooth with use, places it between the forefinger and middle finger, takes aim, and tries to fell as many of the upright beans as possible. Both teams take turns doing this, and the team that fells the most beans is declared the winner. Kungawrhi was so beautiful and graceful as she played Inkawi Bah that the young men of the village would gather in droves to watch her while she frolicked with her friends.

Among her many bachelor admirers was a Keimi, although he kept it a secret from everybody. This weretiger was deeply in love with Kungawrhi, but he believed he had no chance of marrying her when there were so many other eligible human bachelors. His despair nearly drove him out of his mind.

One day the weretiger devised a plan to marry his beloved Kungawrhi. In those days, sometimes people would collect and then dry the footprint of an enemy over a fire in order to cast a spell over them and cause their death. The weretiger decided to do the same with Kungawrhi's footprint—not to kill her of course, but to bring her under his power. He thought if he could make her ill and then present himself as being able to cure her, she would be more favorable towards him. And so he collected her footprint and placed it on the shelf over the fire in his house.

On that same day, Kungawrhi fell ill, and as the days went by she got sicker and sicker. When word spread that the most beautiful and popular girl in the village was sick, everybody became very concerned, and many of the young men and women of the village came to visit their friend and wish her good health. Every day she had dozens of visitors and well-wishers, but she showed no sign of recovery.

The Keimi lad went to see her too, feigning ignorance; but before he went, he cleverly removed Kungawrhi's footprint from the shelf to cool it down. Since her footprint had been removed from the heat, Kungawrhi felt much better while the Keimi was at her house. She even remarked to her father later, "Father, when that lad was in our house to visit me, I felt so much better." Her father replied, "Perhaps you are in love with him; maybe that's why you felt better when you saw him." Kungawrhi was confused. "I'm not aware of being in love with him," she said, but her father did not quite believe her.

Of course, the Keimi had hung Kungawrhi's footprint back over the fire as soon as he got home, so she lapsed back into sickness. Her family performed all the rites and rituals that people suggested they should do to make her better, but nothing worked. Finally, her frantic father proclaimed, "The man who can cure my daughter Kungawrhi shall marry her without any bride-price!" At once, the Keimi volunteered, "I shall cure her, let me try!"

Since nobody had yet realized that he was a Keimi, they allowed him to try to cure her. He quickly went home, and unbeknownst to any one, he shifted her footprint slightly, away from the heat of the fire. Every day, he would visit her and attend to her needs. Biding his time, he slowly and patiently moved the footprint further and further every day, and as he did so, Kungawrhi's condition got better and better. At last, he removed the footprint from the shelf completely and placed it back on the ground, and so Kungawrhi was fully cured.

Now that her health was restored, the Keimi and Kungawrhi soon were married, in keeping with her father's promise. Shortly after, the Keimi took her to his native Keimi home which was far away from her village. Soon after they left Kungawrhi's village, they came upon a big river. The river was in spate, and the angry waters rose terrifyingly high. There was no way for them to cross it under such conditions unless the Keimi did something. He tried and tried to think of a way to cross the turbulent river and still keep his true identity a secret, but finally concluded that there was no other way but to transform into a tiger in front of his new bride. So he told her, "I will turn myself into a tiger; hold on to my tail as tight as you can, and I'll cross the river with you."

The Keimi thus turned into his tiger form, and Kungawrhi held on fast to his tail as instructed. The Keimi growled "Hoo hoo hooo!" and bounded over the river on his powerful legs, with her holding on to him for dear life.

Although they did not see her, a little old lady gathering firewood had observed all this from a distance. She was so shocked at what she had seen that she ran as fast as she could back to the village. She raced straight to the house of Kungawrhi's father, where, terrified and out of breath, she promptly fainted without uttering a single word.

The folks at home were astonished. They revived her and asked, "What is it? What has happened? What is the meaning of this?" but the old lady was not able to say a word. "Somebody give her some buh tui to drink!" they said. Quickly, they took some of the boiled-down rice with the grains strained out and made her drink it. This brought back some of her strength, and she attempted to tell them what she had seen. At first all she could say was, "This… this…. this son of a…. this…" and could not make herself understood. "Give her some more buh tui to drink!" they said, and they gave her some more. This revived her, and she was able to calm down and narrate her story.

"You daughter… your daughter, well, her husband is a weretiger, a Keimi! The two of them came to the river and he turned himself into a tiger and carried her across the churning water. I saw it all! I can't even say how frightened I was, to see that Keimi dashing full speed across the river with your daughter in tow!"

This news greatly disturbed Kungawrhi's father. He immediately went in search of someone who would be brave enough to rescue his daughter. Once again, he proclaimed, "Anyone who is able to rescue my Kungawrhi from the clutches of the Keimi shall marry her without paying any bride-price."

Two brave warriors in the village, Phawthira and his younger brother Hrangchala, rose to the challenge. "We shall rescue her; we shall do as you wish," they said. Before they left for their daunting task, Kungawrhi's father fed them plenty of food and buh zu—rice beer—to fortify them. They also packed a large amount of food for the journey, and set out on their way.

Soon, they reached the village called Vangchhe Tlang. Here Kungawrhi lived with her husband in a hut. After asking around, they found out that he was away hunting. This emboldened them to approach Kungawrhi and reveal their intentions to her. Kungawrhi was afraid that her husband would suddenly return from his hunt, and in order to conceal her visitors, she laid out a woven mat on the floor and rolled the brothers up in the mat. Once they were tightly rolled up, she placed the mat with the brothers inside on a shelf high above the fire, where they would neither be too hot nor easily visible.

Soon afterwards, her husband the Keimi returned from his hunt. As he entered his home and sniffed around, his nose picked up the scent of humans—humans that he hadn't smelled before. He turned to his wife and uttered:

"Hringmi rim nam rum rum!
I smell the aroma of humans in the air!"

But his wife calmly replied, "Well, no wonder, I'm right here!"

The Keimi, not quite convinced, continued to look around, trying to detect the source of the smell.

Seeing this, Phawthira's brother Hrangchala, who was younger and not as courageous as his brother, began to lose his nerve. He was so afraid that he thought he would burst out crying. He tried as hard as he could to hold back, but he shed a few tears in spite of himself. The Keimi happened to see one of the tears fall through the air to the floor. He immediately repeated,

"Kungawrh!
Hringmi rim nam rum rum!
I smell the aroma of humans in the air!
Desolate tears drip-drip-dripping down!"

Kungawrhi bravely replied, "Well, here I am, your human wife. Eat me if you wish!" which quieted him down.

Next morning the Keimi said to his wife, "I am going hunting and will be away for ten nights. Pack me some food." His wife did as she was bid and sent him away with his food. The Keimi, however, did not go hunting as he had said he would. Instead he whiled away his time on the outskirts of the village and returned home before the ten days were up. As he entered his home, once again he said:

"Kungawrh!
Hringmi rim nam rum rum!
I smell the aroma of humans in the air!
Desolate tears drip-drip-dripping down!"

But she gave him the same reply and offered herself up to be eaten if he so wished, and this quieted him again.

The Keimi played the same trick on his wife several times, telling her he would be gone for a long time, and then unexpectedly returning home early, hoping to surprise any unwanted humans in his home. Whenever he left the house, Kungawrhi would give food and drinks to her guests and together the three of them would plan the details of their escape from the Keimi.

One morning, the Keimi called his wife and told her, "Kungawrh, pack me some food. I am going hunting again, but this time, I'll be away only for one night." By this time, Kungawrhi was wise to his ways and understood that he might really be gone for a longer time. She cooked and packed his food, and the Keimi left to go hunting. As soon as he left, Phawthira and Hrangchala emerged from their hiding place, and the three of them hurriedly packed and got ready to leave for their village. They left the pet housecat to keep house and instructed it to spin some cotton on the loom. The three of them packed seeds of fire, seeds of water, seeds of thorns, and seeds of rocks, and sped away.

After some time had passed, the Keimi returned from his hunting trip. He bellowed, "Kungawrh, I am home, open the door for me!" Inside, he could hear the noise of the cotton being spun by the cat and thought it must be his wife. The cat replied, "I'm busy." The Keimi called out once more, "Hurry up and open the door for me!" "I'm too busy," the cat replied again. This made the Keimi so angry that in a fit of temper he broke down the door, shouting, "Be sure that I shall eat you!"

At this, the cat quickly escaped through a hole in the floor and the Keimi was bewildered to find the house empty. He soon realized that Kungawrhi and whoever had come to rescue her had abandoned the house and fled away. This made him terribly angry, and yet at the same time he felt lonely and desperate for his wife. He began pacing up and down the house, thinking of Kungawrhi and her escape.

After some time had passed, the distraught Keimi went to the front of his house and thrashed around in frustration on the platform in front of the door. Then he stopped and simply looked off into the distance, unsure of what to do. But as he scanned the horizon, he chanced to see, far-off, the quick gleam of Kungawrhi's earring.

Kungawrhi and the brothers had already walked as far as seven ram tuk (one ram tuk is the distance between the rice fields of a village and the village itself) when the Keimi happened to see them in the distance. As soon as he recognized them, he let out a roar, stiffened his tail, and charged in their direction at full speed. Since he was such a strong and swift creature, it was not long before he had almost caught up to them.

Meanwhile, there were a god and goddess up in the heavens who were enjoying each other's company, picking out lice from each other's heads. Their leisure was interrupted by a burst of laughter from the god. The goddess asked in surprise, "What is so funny? Did I sit indecently and expose myself?" The god replied, "Indeed, no. I am laughing at the plight of those poor humans being chased by a tiger. They need all the help they can get." His wife, the goddess, said, "Well, then, you must help them!"

And so, the god shouted down to the humans, "Look, he is about to catch up to you. Throw down your seeds of fire!" They did as they were bid, and the land between them and the tiger soon went up in flames. In the time that it took the Keimi to wait out the fire, the humans were able to gain a ram tuk worth of distance. As soon as the fire abated, he let out a deep growl, stiffened his tail, and started chasing after them again.

It was not too long before he almost caught up with them. The god once more came to their rescue and shouted down from heaven, "Throw down your seeds of water!" They did so, and soon there was behind them a body of water so deep and wide that it was impossible to swim across. In the time it took the Keimi to walk around the water, Kungawrhi and her friends managed to gain a ram tuk of distance again.

When the Keimi finally reached the other side of the water, after having taken the long route around it, he let out a deep growl, stiffened his tail, and started chasing after them again. Soon, he was about to catch up to them. The god and goddess shouted with urgency, "Throw down your seeds of thorns!" and they did so. Soon there was a field of thorns between them, and the Keimi had to go on a roundabout path to avoid the thorns. While he did so, Kungawrhi and her friends were once more able to gain another ram tuk's distance.

After the Keimi emerged on the other side of the thorns, he let out a deep growl, stiffened his tail, and started chasing after them yet again. Soon, he was about to catch up to them. At this the divine creatures once more shouted out from above, "Beware! He is about to catch up! Remember the seeds of rocks!" Once again, they did as they were bid and scattered the seeds of rocks, and in the blink of an eye, huge boulders suddenly sprang up between them and the Keimi. The Keimi could not break through these boulders and had to find a way around them, and during this time, Kungawrhi and her friends were able to put between them and their pursuer one more ram tuk.

After the Keimi emerged on the other side of the rocks, he let out a deep growl, stiffened his tail, and started chasing after them once more. After a time, he was about to catch up to them again. Now the humans had no more seeds to scatter, and they began to panic. Finally, Phawthira said, "This cannot go on. I will wait for him here among these reeds, and the two of you must hide on the side of that path there. There is no other way to end this!"

And thus, having no other choice, Phawthira lay in ambush for their pursuer, holding a chemtum—the small, sharp chopper that was the only weapon he had with him. The other two hid as best as they could.

When the Keimi came running in hot pursuit, brave Phawthira was ready for him. The two of them fought a terrible battle that could only end in death for one of them.

After a long and arduous struggle, Phawthira managed to deliver a fatal chop with his blade and the Keimi breathed his last.

It was late in the evening and night would settle soon. After their hard-won victory, they decided to rest for the night and set up camp soon afterwards near a place where three paths converged. However, they were not aware that the place they had chosen to spend the night was an abode of the Khuavang (beings that resemble goblins, and are sometimes regarded as nature's guardians.)

The two brothers devised a plan where they would take turns standing guard throughout the night since this was a very wooded area and might be unsafe. Phawthira took the first shift. As soon as it got dark, the Khuavang emerged from the wood and said:

"Who dares spend the night at these crossroads that belong to us?"

Phawthira replied:

"It is us, Phawthira and Hrangchala,
The ones who gave a sound beating to the ferocious tiger,
The ones who chopped the big cat down near the reeds!"

As soon as the Khuavang heard what he said, they said among themselves, "A voice of courage! A brave voice!" and retreated.

However, the Khuavang could not keep away for long, and soon they were back, asking the same question:

"Who dares spend the night at these crossroads that belong to us?"

Phawthira replied in the same way:

"It is us, Phawthira and Hrangchala,
The ones who gave a sound beating to the ferocious tiger,
The ones who chopped the big cat down near the reeds!"

"A voice of courage! A brave voice!" said the Khuavang and retreated again.

This went on at intervals throughout the night, but Phawthira's voice never wavered, and he never put down his guard, so the Khuavang did not dare to harm him.

As dawn started to break, Phawthira, who had wrestled with a tiger and stood guard all night, became very tired and sleepy. So he woke his brother Hrangchala, and said, "Brother, it is now your turn to stand guard. I am very sleepy and must rest for a while. If the Khuavang come, wake me up at once." Hrangchala agreed and took his position keeping guard over the other two. Phawthira drifted off to sleep soon. Not long after, the Khuavang, as was their usual way, showed themselves and asked:

"Who dares spend the night in these crossroads that belong to us?"

Hrangchala was terrified to encounter the Khuavang. In a weak, tear-filled voice he replied as his brother had:

"It is us, Phawthira and Hrangchala,
The ones who gave a sound beating to the ferocious tiger,
The ones who chopped the big cat down near the reeds!"

But the Khuavang were not to be deceived. Immediately, they noticed the difference, and excitedly exclaimed, "A voice of a coward! A cowardly voice!" They descended upon him, grabbed Kungawrhi and disappeared with her among the bushes nearby.

Phawthira woke up from his exhausted sleep and saw that Kungawrhi was no longer asleep nearby. He called to his brother urgently and asked, "Where is Kungawrhi?"

His brother replied, "The Khuavang have taken her."

"Why didn't you wake me up?" Phawthira asked, and Hrangchala said, "I tried but I could not rouse you."

His brother then asked, "Well then, where did they take her?"

"They took her over there and disappeared among the bushes."

Distraught, the two brothers rushed over to the area and pulled out all the reeds and bushes there. Underneath the foliage they discovered a hole in the ground. When they peered inside it, they found a vast and impressive village. It was the village of the Khuavang.

The two brothers descended into the hole and entered the village. Phawthira shouted to the Khuavang, "Release my Kungawrhi! If you do not, I will throw down my comb!" The Khuavang replied, "We know nothing of your Kungawrhi. By all means, throw down your comb if you wish!"

Hearing this, Phawthira did just as he had threatened and threw down his comb. As soon as he threw it, there was a massive landslide that destroyed an entire street of the village of the Khuavang.

He shouted again, "Release my Kungawrhi! If you don't, I shall drop my hairstick!" to which the Khuavang defiantly replied as before. Phawthira then dropped his hairpin, and immediately another street of the Khuavang village was destroyed by a landslide.

At this point, the Khuavang villagers said, "He is going to destroy our entire village. Give him what he wants!"

The Khuavang then applied some concoctions to their chief's daughter to make her face seem prettier, and handed her to Phawthira. But Phawthira was not fooled and said, "This is not her!" and slammed the girl's body into a nearby wall. "Release my Kungawrhi, or I shall let drop my head scarf!" to which the Khuavang answered as before. However, some of the villagers were very worried and insisted on letting Kungawrhi go. They did not want the entire village to be destroyed if Phawthira created more disastrous landslides.

So they finally relented, and brought her to Phawthira, who prepared to take her home.

The only way to exit the village of the Khuavang was by means of the vine of the Kawi plant, which they could use as a ladder. Kungawrhi and Hrangchala made their way up first, climbing up the vine and out of the hole that led to the Khuavang village. Phawthira went last. However, Phawthira was not aware that his younger brother had bad intentions towards him. Secretly, Hrangchala, who had always stood in the shadow of his bigger, braver, and stronger brother, had been plotting to take Kungawrhi as his own and wanted to get rid of Phawthira. As soon as Kungawrhi and Hrangchala stepped on the ground above the entrance to the village, Hrangchala took his knife and cut the vine that Phawthira was still climbing. He fell to the ground with no hope of escape.. He was stuck in the village of the Khuavang.

Hrangchala and Kungawrhi made their way home, trudging along the paths in the forest until at last, they reached the home of Kungawrhi's father. Amidst the jubilation surrounding her return, Kungawrhi's father immediately started preparations for the upcoming nuptials of his daughter and Hrangchala, as he had given his word that whoever rescued her would be given her hand in marriage. The couple was soon married with much pomp and circumstance. Since Kungawrhi's parents were well advanced in years, they passed on the chieftainship to the newlyweds, and Kungawrhi and her husband became the new chiefs of the village.

Meanwhile, Phawthira, who had no means of escape from the Khuavang village in the foreseeable future, settled into his new life and married a Khuavang lass. He also planted a new Kawi plant and waited patiently for the vine to grow. Time went by, and Phawthira became the father of three children. In the meantime, the Kawi plant he had nurtured started to flourish, its vine growing longer and stronger upon the ground until it extended up the rock face and towards the entrance of the village.

He knew it would soon be possible for him to escape the village, and he began to test the vine for strength every day, climbing up as high as it would hold him. But every time he started climbing, his children would cry out, "Father, where are you going? Wait for us, will you, we want to climb up too!" and this would make him postpone his plans for another day.

This went on for quite some time, until one day, he decided to go about it a different way. He told his children he would boil some eggs as a treat for them, which excited them greatly. Then he instructed them, "Do not call me anymore until the eggs are cooked," and went climbing up the vine again. However, the eggs got done quickly and his children started calling him again before he could make his escape. "Father, climb down from your vine, the eggs are cooked," they said, and he once more had to heed their calls.

He then devised a new plan. He took the stone mortar that was used for crushing salt, and put that on the fire. He gave them strict instructions, "Do not call me until this is cooked." His children kept checking the mortar by prodding the stone, but it remained firm. It didn't seem to get cooked no matter how many times they checked. This gave Phawthira enough time to climb the vine all the way to the top and out through the entrance of the hole, finally leaving his children behind.

As soon as he managed to escape from the Khuavang village, Phawthira headed straight towards his old village. There, he saw that Hrangchala and Kungawrhi were in the midst of hosting a feast of merit, a ceremony called Khuangchawi. The couple were perched atop a big drum, reveling in the moment. Phawthira went straight to them and in one fell swoop struck down his brother, and then proceeded to cut his body into three pieces.

The people were aghast. "Ehh ehh ehhh!" they cried in consternation. "Why has this man come and killed our chief without any provocation! Capture him and kill him too!"

Phawthira was captured and was about to be put to death as punishment. But he said, "Wait, wait, hear me out. Before you kill me, I have something to say." The people of the village considered this and said, "It is right; if he has something to say, he must be given a chance to say it," and so they listened. He proceeded to narrate the events that had happened:

"This woman, Kungawrhi, was rescued by us from her Keimi husband who then pursued us. We used seeds of fire, water, thorns, and rocks but nothing could stop him. There was no other way out, so I fought a fierce battle with him and managed to kill him. Then, as we stopped for the night at a place haunted by Khuavang, they tried to disturb us, but I kept guard and kept them at bay all night long. When Hrangchala took over from me, he could not keep us safe; he allowed Kungawrhi to be captured by the Khuavang."

He then continued to relate all the details of everything that had happened at Khuavang village, up to the point where the vine was cut by Hrangchala, leaving Phawthira to his fate among the Khuavang, and how after many years had passed, he was finally able to come home and seek justice.

Thus Phawthira told the villagers that it was in fact he who had rescued Kungawrhi from the clutches of not just her Keimi husband but from the Khuavang as well. Since her father had promised his daughter's hand in marriage to whoever rescued her, he concluded that Kungawrhi should rightfully be his wife. "My brother Hrangchala cheated me of what was rightfully mine. This deceit and injustice so angered me that I had no choice but to kill him!" he told the people. Kungawrhi, too, confirmed all this.

All the villagers and even Kungawrhi's own parents agreed with his reasoning. "If that was how it happened, then what he says is correct!" they said, and absolved him of all guilt.

Phawthira then married Kungawrhi, and together they ruled over the people as chiefs of their village from that day on.

The Story of Chawngtinleri

Once upon a time, in the village of Seipui, there lived a beautiful maiden named Chawngtinleri. Her parents had died when she was young, so she lived with her older brother, Liana. The two siblings had grown up with no one to depend on except each other, and the love between them was very strong.

Chawngtinleri was so beautiful that she had attracted the attention of one of the Lasi, the faeries or spirits of the hills. The name of this Lasi was Lalchungnunga, and he was a king among the faerie-people—the King of Tan, which is one of the highest hills in Mizoram. Lalchungnunga had fallen so much in love with Chawngtinleri that he was resolved to marry her.

Sometimes, in those days, the Lasi would choose certain humans and bestow special favour upon them. These humans were blessed with superior hunting skills, and unlike most people, they were able to communicate with the Lasi. Such people were called "Lasi zawl". There was one Lasi in particular who had bestowed her favour on many: she was a lovely maiden named Tinchhingi, and she loved to participate in the sport of the human hunters. Tinchhingi was from Tan Hill, too, and she was a very popular spirit among the humans. Those she favoured became so enamored with her that they composed songs in her honour. It was from those who had been possessed by Tinchhingi that everyone near and far soon came to know about Lalchungnunga's love for Chawngtinleri.

The beautiful Chawngtinleri had every young man in her human village in thrall. They would fall all over each other trying to get her to notice them. At the same time, the Lasi were trying to figure out how to win Chawngtinleri over for Lalchungnunga. They began by trying to persuade Chawngtinleri's brother Liana to give his sister's hand in marriage to their king. But Liana was greatly distressed by the idea of letting his sister marry a non-human spirit.

Still, the Lasi would not give up. They tried everything in their power to get him to change his mind.

One night, as Chawngtinleri's brother Liana was sleeping, another beautiful Lasi maiden named Liansailovi appeared in his dreams to flirt with him. Seductively, Liansailovi got him to rest his head on her lap, and began to stroke him lovingly. "Liana," she said to him softly, "if you will give us your sister Chawngtinleri for our King Lalchungnunga's wife, you will never want for anything for the rest of your life. Chawngtinleri, too, shall be given all the comforts she desires, and she will reign as queen over all the animals."

However much Liana wished that Liansailovi's caresses would continue, he could not agree to what she proposed. He awoke with a start, and marveled at the vividness of his dream.

The next night, Liansailovi appeared in his dream again. "Liana, Liana, let your sister marry our king," she said. "We will make you a great warrior, a powerful hunter of animals, and a conqueror of men. We will provide you with plenty of food and wine, and we will ensure that all your descendants become great warriors, as well. You will spend all the days of your life in luxury."

But again, Liana refused.

On the third night, the Lasi came in full force, determined to overcome Liana's objections with great promises and artful arguments. They appeared in his dreams, all of them at once, and begged him, "Liana! Please give us your permission to take your sister to be the bride of our lord, Lalchungnunga. Chawngtinleri shall be given whatever comforts she desires, and we will make her queen over all the animals. You may ask for anything you wish as her bride-price. We shall provide you with beasts numerous enough to fill an entire valley: our finest male boars, whose tusks are as long as the beam of a weaving loom, and our biggest wild sial, too. If you accept, we will be so grateful that we will even present you with a gun and a basketful of bullets." When Liana heard all this, he became very tempted. He imagined what it would feel like to be a warrior powerful enough to kill even the most fearsome beasts of the jungle. Finally, the temptation proved too much for him, and he agreed.

The next morning, he awoke with the dream fresh in his mind. At first he wasn't sure whether to believe it had really happened. He became filled with remorse at having given in to the Lasi. He tried to comfort himself, saying, "It wasn't real! It was just a dream!" Still, he didn't dare to tell anyone. He was terrified that the Lasi would come and snatch his sister. He began guarding her constantly.

With Liana always protecting her, the Lasi could not take Chawngtinleri easily, but they were there watching over her all the time, looking for a chance to grab her.

One morning, Chawngtinleri was grinding rice with a mortar and pestle on the front porch of the house. Her brother, who was inside the house, suddenly heard the sound of the wooden mortar falling, and his sister's voice crying in panic, "Ka u Lian! Brother Liana!" He immediately ran outside, crying, "Chawngtinler!" but she was nowhere to be seen. The wooden pestle where she had been grinding just a few moments before now contained a gun and many bullets. He stared at it in horror. He looked around in vain for his sister, but then he remembered his dream, and he was sure the Lasi had kidnapped her.

In the days that followed, he wandered the hills in hopes of seeing her, but she was nowhere to be found. He was inconsolable.

Wherever he went, he noticed the animals acting strangely. They would stop right in front of him, presenting themselves as easy targets. But Liana, suspecting that these were part of the bounty offered by the Lasi as Chawngtinleri's bride-price, refused to shoot them.

One day, he decided to go hunting with his friends on Tan Hill. Liana wandered off the paths to explore all the ravines and crevices of the hill, hoping to catch sight of Chawngtinleri, but he found no sign of her. Finally, disheartened, he gave up his search and sat on top of a rock. He took a leaf and played it (the art of making music with a leaf was popular in those days) and he started singing:

"While I wander lonely and despairing,
how do you pass your days,
My soulmate, my beloved Chawngi?"

Hearing the song of her brother, Chawngtinleri replied likewise in song;

"While you wander lonely and despairing, I do nothing
But cry every day, between the hills, Lurhpui and Tan."

Although he could hear her voice singing back to him, Liana could not see her anywhere, and he went home feeling miserable.

When the Lasi saw that Liana was refusing to kill any of the animals they offered him, they became very concerned. One night, they sent Chawngtinleri to appear in his dream. With tears streaming down her face, she spoke to him in his dream: "Brother Liana, from now on you must shoot the animals provided for you. Why are you so upset? It is with your own permission that they have taken me."

From then on, Liana started killing the game that came his way. The Lasi appeared to him again in his dreams, and told him, "Do not worry about your sister. Between Lurhpui Hill and Tan Hill, your sister reigns as queen, feasting and making merry, and she doesn't ever have to do any work at all."

Every day, Liana found himself worrying less and less about his sister's fate. He was hunting again, and enjoying it. Chawngtinleri, invisible, would often drive the animals toward her brother so that they became easy prey. He was extremely successful, bringing home all sorts of game every day.

The Lasi had not forgotten the wild boar they had promised Liana as part of Chawngtinleri's bride-price. Again they appeared in his dream. "Tomorrow, we shall give you the wild boar we promised to you," they said, and told him where to lie in wait. As dawn broke the next morning, Liana proceeded to the edge of forest to wait for the boar as instructed. The Lasi enthusiastically drove the huge animal towards the place where Liana waited, poised and ready to shoot.

"Go, Boar! Go toward Liana, so that his fame as a hunter may spread far and wide!" they sang to the boar. Some of them even pushed it from behind. Liana, hearing these sounds, was filled with joyous anticipation.

Soon, Liana caught sight of the magnificent wild boar, trampling along the ground in slow, heavy steps. Its tusk was as big as the wooden bar of the weaving loom. Thinking about how famous he would become once he had felled such an enormous beast, Liana was filled with glee, and he grinned in happiness. As soon as he smiled, the wild boar made a loud noise—"Haak!"—and ran away. Liana nearly wept with regret at the lost opportunity.

The Lasi berated him, saying, "We shall try to drive him toward you once more. But this time, don't show your teeth!" This time, the wild boar was more reluctant to move, and the Lasi had to prod him harder. They sang to him, as before: "Go, Boar! Go toward Liana, so that his fame as a hunter may spread far and wide!" Some of them pushed the boar from behind while others pulled him forward by the ear.

Finally, they managed to lead him towards the place where Liana stood ready and waiting to strike. Unfortunately, just as had happened before, thoughts of his future glory on accomplishing the feat once more filled Liana with delight, and as he raised his gun to shoot the animal, he could not help grinning. Just as had happened before, as soon as the boar saw the gleam of his teeth, it said "Haak!" and ran away again.

Liana didn't manage to shoot anything else all day, and he went home a failure.

Once more, the Lasi appeared in Liana's dream. "Tomorrow, we shall try to present you the boar one last time. Do not show your teeth again. If you fail tomorrow, we won't be able to lead the animal to you anymore," they warned him.

The next morning, Liana went into the forest at daybreak, determined to kill the boar. He lay in wait for the animal, concealed behind a tree. As before, he heard low grunting as the boar approached, and as before, he heard the Lasi driving the animal towards him, singing to it. He was determined not to let his face show any emotion this time. The voices of the Lasi grew closer and stronger, until they were so close that he could have joined in their song: "Go, Boar! Go toward Liana, so that his fame as a hunter may spread far and wide!"

As he watched, the enormous brute came tramping down the path with its heavy, plodding gait. He raised his gun and took careful aim. But as his finger tightened on the trigger, he could not help thinking again of the fame and glory he would achieve, and yet again, he grinned. "Haak!" cried the boar, and in the blink of an eye, it disappeared into the woods.

Liana couldn't believe that he had missed his chance again. He could only stare helplessly at the boar's tracks.

The Lasi said to him, "Liana, perhaps that boar was not destined to be yours. It won't be possible for us to drive it to you again!"

After its escape, the boar travelled very far away to a new pasture in Tawihzo, too far for the Lasi to bring it back. It was such a huge beast that its tracks made deep marks on the paths in the forest. Legend has it that, in later years, this was the same beast that killed the famous warrior Khualtungamtawna.

A few nights later, the Lasi once more appeared in Liana's dream. "Tomorrow we will present you with our biggest sial, the one with the most magnificent horn. But you mustn't smile or show your teeth! If you do, you won't be able to shoot it." The next morning, happy and carefree, Liana set out towards the valley where the Lasi had instructed him to wait. He made careful arrangements along the trail of the sial, setting up a vantage point from which to aim and shoot at it. The Lasi made themselves visible to Liana now, and they drove the reluctant sial towards him. As they pushed and prodded the sial from behind, they chanted and sang, "Go, Sial! Go toward Liana, so that his fame as a hunter may spread far and wide!" Listening to their singing voices, Liana was filled with such happiness that he almost smiled again. Soon, he could see them approaching closer and closer. The sial was more enormous than he could ever have imagined. Its huge horns arced out from its head, splendid and lustrous. There seemed to be a rainbow etched between those horns; the animal had a magnetism that mesmerized the beholder. The thick, rippling folds of skin on its forehead and chest gave it a look of grandeur.

Liana had never seen anything like it before. He stood rooted to the spot, not moving a muscle, just gazing in awed fascination. He was enchanted by the beauty of the magical creature, and he stared in thrilled rapture at the sight before his eyes. His heart pounded in his breast at the thought that he would be the huntsman to have brought down this majestic beast. But as it passed the spot where he stood waiting, he stood transfixed, unable to do anything but watch. By the time he had gathered his wits and tried to aim his gun, the sial had moved too far away.

The Lasi spoke to him then, and berated him, reminding him how difficult it had been for them to capture it. But they chased the animal and captured it once more, and again they led it to Liana, singing all the while.

This time, Liana took careful aim, determined not to miss his opportunity. The animal was stubbornly refusing to move, no matter how much the Lasi poked and prodded it from behind. The oldest among the Lasi, who was determined to make the kill as easy as possible for Liana, was pushing the animal with all his might. As they came closer, this Lasi elder pushed so hard that as he exerted himself, he accidentally farted. Liana found this so funny that he could not help laughing out aloud. The old Lasi, angry at being laughed at, gave the sial a smack on its behind, and the animal ran to its freedom, once more robbing Liana of his chance at fame.

With the passing of time, the relationship between the Lasi and Liana improved and became more and more cordial. Although he had succeeded in killing neither the enormous boar nor the magical sial, they gave him many other animals which he did kill, and he did become known as a successful huntsman.

The Lasi even permitted Chawngtinleri to visit her home occasionally. When she did come, she brought her baby with her; but she kept it hidden from sight, and if she had to go out to do some chore or to answer the call of nature, she would warn everyone not to look at it. But precisely because of this warning, people became curious. One day, when Chawngtinleri had stepped outside to go to the toilet, the villagers stole a quick glimpse at her baby. When they did, they got a shock. Chawngtinleri's baby was like no other baby they had ever seen. It had a human body, but the head of a goat!

The Lasi became very angry at Chawngtinleri for allowing human eyes to see her baby. They forbade her from ever visiting her home again, saying that she had betrayed the secret of their true forms. With no hope of visiting her home again, Chawngtinleri became so lonely that she did not know what to do. No matter how long she had stayed with the Lasi, her misery did not diminish. Finally, desperate for her to stop pining and adjust to her life with King Lalchungnunga, the Lasi took her eyes and twisted them in her head, so that they were turned vertically. After they had done this, her loneliness slowly abated, and she stopped missing her fellow humans.

Chawngtinleri remained queen of all the beasts of the forests. She would sit in the valley between Lurh Hill and Tan Hill and weave. The martins from the forest would come and help her with her loom.

And so the Lasi were regarded as being very honourable, and faithful to the promises that they made. They were held in such high regard that for a time, the Chhakchhuak tribe believed that Lurh Hill and Tan Hill were sacred, and worshipped them.

Chawngtinleri was revered as the queen of all animals ever after, but she is most closely associated with the boar.

The Story of Chawngchilhi

A long time ago, there was a maiden named Chawngchilhi. She lived with her young sister and her father as her mother had died when the girls were very young.

Now, it so happened that every time the family had a new rice harvest, birds would come and peck away at the grain before they had a chance to gather it up. It was decided that Chawngchilhi and her sister would go every day to the rice field to guard the crops from being eaten by the pesky birds. Their father was a good man who doted on his daughters. Every day, he lovingly wrapped cooked rice and meat delicacies in plantain leaves for the sisters to eat at midday while they worked hard to guard their crops.

However, even though they always left home with plenty of food for their midday meal, the younger sister kept growing thinner and thinner. Soon her father noticed and started to worry. One day, he called her aside and asked, "My precious daughter, I make sure to pack food for you and your sister every day for fear that you will go hungry, so why is it that you are getting so thin?" But the little girl would not say why. This made her father even more worried, and he kept asking her the reason for her frail and thin appearance. Finally, the little girl, in a small and fearful voice said, "Father, I cannot tell you why, for if I do, my sister will be angry at me and beat me."

Now her father was truly alarmed and forced his daughter to tell him the truth, coaxing and threatening her until she finally said, "There is a python near our field, and my sister and that snake have fallen in love. Sister makes me call out to the python at midday, and he comes slithering up to her. They take off their garments and spend time together every day, and afterwards they eat the meal you pack for us. I am always too scared of the python to eat any food, and that is why I have grown thin."

Horrified and angry to hear of such happenings, her father devised a plan to put an end to it. One day, he told Chawngchilhi that she should rest at home, and he would take her place at the field. Chawngchilhi did not want to miss a day with her beloved python, and tried to find a way to go, saying "Father you are older and will get tired guarding the field in the hot sun. Let me go instead." But her father insisted on going, and she was helpless in the face of his determination. Reluctantly, she agreed to her father's wishes. And so, her father and sister set off towards their rice field.

When it got to be the lovers' usual meeting time, the father asked his daughter to summon the python as she always did for her sister. Obediently, the young girl did so:

"Oh, Chawngchilhi's lover,
Mother pleads for you to come,
Father pleads for you to come."

As soon as the python heard the melodious voice of the girl, he slithered towards them, chanting back his amorous declarations:

"I will come to you shortly,
I am preening my hair for you,
Donning my headwrap to look nice for you,
Ready to rest upon your bosom like a necklace."

The python started to slither from the field towards them, puffed up with vanity and anticipation, excited to meet Chawngchilhi and spend time with her as always. To his shock, he saw not Chawngchilhi, but her father, who was livid with rage.

When the father realized that his daughter had indeed been telling him the truth, it made him even angrier. He had been ready and waiting for this moment, and as soon as he saw the python, he took his chempui—a sharp blade, like a machete—and slashed right through the middle of his body without a moment's hesitation, cutting him in two, and killing him in an instant.

At home, neither father nor daughter told Chawngchilhi about the day's events.

The following day, the two sisters once again set out towards the fields. When the hot noon sun climbed high and it was time for their midday rest, Chawngchilhi asked her little sister to summon the python. Without protest, her sister did as she was told. This time, however, there was nobody to answer her. Chawngchilhi became distraught. She missed her lover and wept for him, to no avail.

As she cried, she lamented:

"Whose sharp blade did you meet, my beloved?
Was it a blade from the north?
Or was it one from the south?"

As she uttered those words in anguish, the spirit of the python replied to her:

"I did not chance upon a sharp blade from the south,
Nor did I encounter one from the north,
It was indeed your own father's blade that I met."

Chawngchilhi was filled with shock and despair at hearing these words and wept bitterly. Later that evening, she trudged home disconsolately with her sister. Upon reaching home, they found that their father had dozed off to sleep with his chempui in his hand. When he heard them returning he awoke. Chawngchilhi could not hide her sorrow at the loss of her lover, and the father and daughter started to exchange heated words. In the heat of the moment, her father, still enraged at his daughter's behavior, struck her with his sharp chempui.

As Chawngchilhi lay dying, it became apparent that she was pregnant with the python's children—and that it was almost time for her to give birth. As the life left her body, these offspring left her too; dozens of tiny snakelets crawled out of her belly, heading towards the forest. Her father, quick to react, took his chempui and quickly killed all the snakes as fast as he saw them—except one, which managed to escape his sharp blade.

This lone snakelet slithered off towards the forest. There it grew big and in time, became a menace to the villagers. It would destroy their crops and devour their livestock; eventually, it even started to prey on the village children and eat them. It had a secret cave where it hid.*

There was a little old woman who knew exactly where the cave was located, but when they asked her, she said, "I will not tell anyone where the cave is unless you promise me that you will give me the choicest part of the snake meat when you kill it." So, they promised her they would, and she told them where the cave was. They then set a trap near the entrance of its cave and managed to capture it. They put a noose around its neck and the entire village came together to try to pull the snake out of its cave. Men, women,

---

* This cave later became known as Rulchawm Puk or Chawngchilhi Puk; it still exists to this day.

and children all took a grip on the rope and heaved with all their might.

The snake was so big that even after they had managed to pull out quite a long part of it out of the cave, it arrogantly bellowed:

"No matter how much you pull me,
My tail still extends to the other edge of the horizon."

After a considerable time had passed, the villagers grew so tired of trying to pull the snake out of its cave that they simply cut up the part of it that they could see. They distributed its meat among the entire village, but they did not keep their promise to the little old woman; they gave her only the head of the snake.

She took it home and tried to cook it in a stew for the morning. She cooked it all night long, since she had a guest who was staying with her and wanted to prepare a nice meal for him. In the morning, when she went to check on her stew by poking at it with her cooking prong, the snake head said, "Be careful not to poke my eyes!" so she decided it needed a little more time to cook. Yet even after she had cooked it again for a length of time, it remained tough and inedible, so she threw it out of the house.

As night drew close, all the cocks around the lady's house began to crow, "Tee-tee-eek-eek, let the visitor leave the village!" and so the little old lady urged her guest to get out of the village as soon as possible. As soon as he went, there was a tremendous earthquake, and every household that had eaten the snake meat was destroyed; only the little old lady's hut remained standing.

The snake head which she had thrown away turned into a gourd plant that produced one enormous gourd, as big as the old lady's hut.

Legend has it that Chhurbura†, another folk hero of the Mizo people, used to ask people to guess how many seeds the giant gourd had. Chhura was often regarded as a simpleton because of his unconventional ways and his sense of humor. Many people guessed, but he said that all their guesses were wrong, and finally they asked him to tell the right answer. Chhurbura replied, "As big as it is, it has only one seed." When the skeptical villagers split open the gourd, they saw in amazement that it had, indeed, only a single seed.

Today, people use the expression "the one gourd seed that Chhura knew about" to convey a situation where an unlikely person knows a secret that nobody else does.

† Chhurbura is the hero of many Mizo folk stories. He is sometimes portrayed as a cunning trickster, other times as a complete idiot, and often as a curious mixture of both. I have included one short Chhura story in this book; for many more, see the work of B. Lalthangliana, Lalhmachhuana Zofa, and others.

The Story of Ngaiteii

One day Ngaiteii and her grandmother were digging up taro in their jhum for their evening meal. At the bottom of their jhum was a large, deep pool, a widening of the river Tiau. This was the pool where Ngaiteii's father had drowned some years before, and it was believed that her father's spirit lived inside it.

It was a hot and sunny day, and their work was very tiring. Ngaiteii, especially, kept getting thirsty, and soon the gourd-flask of water was empty. Her grandmother would go to the pool to refill the gourd; but she soon grew tired, because Ngaiteii kept drinking it up and the pool was far away. So she said, "Ngaite, it is a bit of a walk to the pond and I am exhausted. Why don't you refill the gourd yourself this time? But be careful: when you reach the pond, you must not exclaim 'E Khai!' no matter what you see there."

Ngaiteii left for the pool to refill her gourd. When she reached the pool and looked down, she saw that the water was dark and transparent. It filled her with awe. Forgetting her grandmother's warning, she exclaimed, "E Khai!" in amazement. The moment she uttered these words, her father's spirit rose from the pool and grabbed her.

After a while, Ngaiteii's grandmother started to wonder why she had not returned. She waited and waited, and finally decided to walk down to the pool to see what was keeping her. She hoped to meet her along the way; surely, Ngaiteii would have refilled her gourd and be on her way back by now. But she did not see her anywhere. Confused and panicked, her grandmother began walking faster.

After a while, she met a deer couple. She asked them if they had seen Ngaiteii, and they replied:

"See her we did,
But beyond the mighty waters, beyond the Tiau river
Ngaiteii's father has taken her away."

Ngaiteii's grandmother quickly hurried on until she met a partridge couple. She asked them if they had seen Ngaiteii, and they replied:

"See her we did,
But beyond the mighty waters, beyond the Tiau river
Ngaiteii's father has taken her away."

Ngaiteii's grandmother went on, still looking for her. By and by, she reached the pool at the bottom of their jhum . Peering inside, she saw Ngaiteii at the bottom of the pool. She was preparing the evening meal.

Ngaiteii's grandmother, overjoyed to see her, shouted "Ngaite, I'm coming to get you!" and jumped into the water.

Ngaiteii was very happy to see her grandmother and hugged her tight. Her grandmother asked, "And where is your father's spirit?" Ngaiteii replied, "He has gone to his jhum field. He will return in the evening."

In the evening, the spirit of Ngaiteii's father came home in the form of a large python. A short while later, he transformed himself into human form. Ngaiteii's grandmother asked him, "May I please take Ngaiteii home?"

Her father replied, "Yes you may take her home. However, she must return to me soon. I have missed her and would like her to stay with me from now on." With his permission and a promise to return, Ngaiteii and her grandmother emerged from the pool and went home, relieved.

But as the days went by, Ngaiteii became more and more reluctant to return to her father, despite the promise she had made. She continued to stay with her grandmother and refused to go back to the pool. This irked her father, who made the waters of the pool flood towards her village. As the flood swirled and churned angrily towards her house, the waves seemed to call out ominously, "Ngai, Ngai!" demanding that Ngaiteii come back.

The villagers watched the waters rise and slowly start to submerge their streets. "Our village is being flooded and it's Ngaiteii's fault!" they exclaimed. As the sun moved across the sky, the waters showed no sign of abating. The villagers began to panic, crying out, "E Khai! Our entire village is going to be submerged! Throw Ngaiteii's puan into the water!" So they got Ngaiteii's clothes and threw them into the rising water. This made the flood recede for a little while.

However, it wasn't long before the water started to rise again. The villagers cried, "We are going to drown! What shall we do?" Somebody said, "Throw Ngaiteii's comb into the water!" and they did so. Again, the waters were mollified—but only for a short while. Soon, they started to rise again.

In order to calm the flood, the villagers threw in Ngaiteii's bangles, her necklaces, her woven baskets, her loin-loom, and anything else they could find that belonged to her. Each time they threw something in, the waters receded for a short while; but each time they rose again, more violently than before.

"Ngai, Ngai, Ngai!" cried the angry red water. Soon, the villagers saw that their village was in danger of being completely swept away. They had run out of Ngaiteii's possessions to appease the flood. In the end, it became a choice between sacrificing Ngaiteii or the lives of all the villagers. Reluctantly, they decided to give her up. They took the heartbroken Ngaiteii's hands, led her to the edge, and threw her into the heart of the churning waters.

As soon as they had done so, the flood subsided.

Afterwards, everyone mourned the loss of Ngaiteii. They cried:

"Ngaite! (sniff, sniff)
You have suffered the fury of the southern wind
The rage of the heaven's rains
Ngaite (sniff, sniff)."

The Story of Tualvungi & Zawlpala

A long, long time ago, there lived a very handsome man named Zawlpala, and his beautiful wife Tualvungi. They were deeply in love. One day, a short time after they were married, they sat down together on the platform near the entrance of their hut, searching for lice in each other's hair—a favourite pastime in those days. Just then, a rich vai merchant named Phuntiha happened to pass by and see them. (Vai was a term that the Mizos used to refer to non-Mizos, the people from the plains down below.)

When Phuntiha espied Tualvungi, he thought she was very beautiful indeed. He asked Zawlpala, "Is that your wife?"

Now, Zawlpala, who was very proud of his wife's beauty, answered in jest, "No, she is my sister."

"Well then," said the haughty Phuntiha, "I will make her my wife. In return, what will you demand as bride-price?"

Zawlpala had no idea how immensely rich Phuntiha was. Believing that he would never be able to fulfill his demands, he replied, "For bride-price I demand bison, enough animals to tie on every post and pillar I have; beads and necklaces, enough to break my clothes-post with their weight; daos, enough to cover my thatched walls when I hang them; and woven cloths, to break the string outside on which I hang my clothes."

To his surprise, Phuntiha replied, "So it shall be; I will bring those things to you." If only Zawlpala had admitted his joke then, and confessed the truth, disaster would have been averted. But alas, he remained quiet.

So, Phuntiha went back to his home and started preparations for his nuptials, assisted by his entire village. When the preparations were over, he and his friends went back to Tualvungi's village. Tualvungi, who happened to be outside just then, saw in the distance a great company of men led by Phuntiha, and her heart leapt in her mouth. She uttered in trepidation:

"There in the distance, far in the horizon,
He comes leading a great herd of bison,
Burdened with loads of woven cloths;
Say, 'She is with child',
My beloved Zawlpala."

She wanted her husband to calm her, to soothe her fears; but it seemed Zawlpala was at a loss as to how to handle the situation, and he did nothing to stop the party. Phunitha and his friends came closer and closer, and soon reached Zawlpala's house. Without further ado, they began piling gifts in front of him, all the items that he had demanded as Tualvungi's bride-price. Zawlpala watched aghast as the men led the bison forward and tied them to each pillar and post in sight. They brought out the daos and hung them on every available space on the walls. They displayed woven cloths and hung them on the clothes-line until it snapped. And they offered beads, so many that the strings of the clothes-post broke under the weight.

Zawlpala regretted his foolish mistake terribly, but there was nothing he could do. He watched helplessly as Tualvungi was led away by Phuntiha's men. He stood rooted to the ground as they walked away and disappeared over the horizon, moaning to himself, "I have made a mistake! Woe is me!" He was engulfed by loneliness.

So too was Tualvungi. She followed the men silently, having no means of resisting them.

Zawlpala's loneliness was so great that before much time had elapsed, he found himself unable to resist the urge to go to Tualvungi's new home in Phuntiha's village, where he stayed as a guest in their house. Tualvungi warned Zawlpala to be very careful while he stayed there. "If Phuntiha offers you a meal which he does not offer to others, do not eat it," she cautioned him.

One day, while Tualvungi was away collecting firewood, Phuntiha offered Zawlpala fire-roasted yams and zufang, or rice beer. Zawlpala, figuring that this didn't really count as a meal, innocently accepted the offering. When she came back, she asked him, "What did you eat today?"

"Roasted yam and zufang," Zawlpala replied.

"Oh no! Why did you eat that?!" Tualvungi replied in horror. "Consider yourself lucky if you make it home to your own bed before you die. Run, run home!"

Zawlpala speedily ran home. The moment he reached home, he was wracked with a severe stomach ache. Soon afterwards, he died. The village mourned him and buried him, performing all the necessary rituals and rites. In those days, when somebody died, a sacrifice was offered for the dead, so that the spirit of the slain animals would accompany the departed to other world. Such sacrifices were performed for Zawlpala, and the skulls of the slain bison were displayed all around his grave. After a while, his mourners said, "Somebody should go and summon Tualvungi and inform her that her Zawlpala has died." So they began looking for a messenger to call Tualvungi.

A crab came, and they asked him, "Will you be able to call Tualvungi?"

"Yes," said the crab.

"How will you call her?" they asked.

The crab replied, "I will say, 'Ai, ai'."

So they said, "He does not know how to call her," and they trod on him and trampled him to the ground. It is said that from that day onward, the crab has walked sideways.

Next, a choak—that is, a raven—came. "Will you be able to call Tualvungi?" they asked him.

"Yes," said the choak.

"How will you call her?"

The choak replied, "I will say, 'Ak, ak'."

Irritated, they said, "You don't know anything!" and they poured black dye all over him. It is said that from that day onwards, the choak has been black.

Then, a tlaiberh—a red-vented bulbul—came, and they asked him if he would be the messenger, and how he would summon Tualvungi.

"I will summon her by saying, 'Berek berek, kuai kin lut'," the tlaiberh said.

They decided that he spoke nothing but nonsense. "You don't know anything!" they said, and speared him on the pointed fence, drawing blood. It is said that from that day onwards, the tlaiberh's crissum feathers have been red.

Lastly, a vahui—a wood-pigeon—came, and they asked him, "Huia, would you be able to summon Tualvungi?"

"Certainly," replied the vahui. "I will say: Hui, hui e, I say hui hui e, far, far away has Zawlpala died, let Tualvungi pay her respects."

"Well done," they said, and decided that he was the best messenger to send to Tualvungi. So they fed him with rice and meat and sent him on his way.

The vahui went on his mission, flying across the sky to the place where Tualvungi lived. Once there, he saw Tualvungi weaving in her house, and he perched atop a branch of a tree near her. Then he began to sing:

"Hui e, hui e,
Far, far away has Zawlpala died,
Let Tualvungi pay her respects,
I say hui, hui e."

Mizo houses used to be built with a platform near the entrance called a luhkapui, which had no roof. When she heard the bird's song, Tualvungi responded, "If it is me you are addressing, fly down to the pillar on our luhkapui and sing your song again."

The vahui flew down as requested, and sang his song again. But Tualvungi was still not convinced. "If you are truly talking to me," she said, "fly down and perch atop this loom of mine where I am weaving, and tell me again."

The bird once again did as she requested, and sang his song a third time. At this, Tualvungi remembered her manners as a hostess. "For you, weary messenger," she said, and she offered the vahui some meat and rice, and sent him flying back home after he was full.

Tualvungi now also planned to go back home, but her husband Phuntiha would not allow it. To prevent her from slipping away in his absence, he laid a trap for her. He placed a very sharp dao facing upwards just near the door. When he was away, Tualvungi planned a stealthy escape; but she did not see the dao, and stepped on it on her way out, cutting a deep gash in her foot. But Tualvungi did not let that stop her; going over to her woven basket, she opened the cover and took out her freshly woven cloth, tore it up and bandaged her foot. She also took some other important possessions of hers and proceeded on her journey.

As she travelled on, she came across a group of young boys and girls playing with kawi—the large, bean-like seeds with which Mizo children love to play games. She asked:

"Little children shooting kawi, way over there,
Pray, tell me, have you seen the grave of Zawlpala,
My beloved Zawlpala's grave?"

They replied in a chorus:

"Around Zawlpala's grave
Lies a bed of tuangtuah flowers in bloom,
Bison heads displayed in a row."

The grateful Tualvungi threw some kawi their way, and the children scrambled after them. She went on. After travelling over a long distance, she came across another group of children watching over a herd of sial. So, she asked them:

"Little children watching sial, way over there,
Pray, tell me, have you seen the grave of Zawlpala,
My beloved Zawlpala's grave?"

The little children replied:

"Around Zawlpala's grave
Lies a bed of tuangtuah flowers in bloom,
Bison heads displayed in a row."

In gratitude, she threw across a thick vine to be used as a rope for the sial, and the children scrambled after it. She went on, in search of her beloved's grave, and finally she found it. She wept, heartbroken, over Zawlpala's resting place. A little old woman came and tried to comfort her, but Tualvungi was inconsolable. She said to the old woman, "Kapi, do not try to console me; instead, please kill me, and you shall have all my clothes. I will not survive this pain."

The old woman replied, "Let it be so."

With that, together, they dug up Zawlpala's grave, and found that Zawlpala's remains had been reduced to a skeleton. Tualvungi knelt to lay herself down beside him. "Zawlpala," she said, "make room, there is no space for Tualvungi." The bones of Zawlpala arranged themselves to make way for Tualvungi, and the little old woman killed her then.*

In the meantime, Phuntiha had also come in pursuit of Tualvungi, but by the time he reached her, she was already dead. In his grief, he lay down beside the dead lovers and killed himself. But Tualvungi and Zawlpala turned themselves into butterflies and flew away. Then Phuntiha turned himself into a butterfly as well, and flew off in pursuit. That is why, even now, we often see a butterfly couple flying together with a third butterfly chasing after them.

---

* Twin graves, said to be Tualvungi's and Zawlpala's, can be seen in the village of Phulpui, about halfway between Aizawl and Thenzawl.

The Story of the Beginning of the World

The Creation of the Earth

Eons ago, in time immemorial, a goddess named Khuazing-nu created the earth. To make it cool and habitable, she created all sorts of vegetation, and to nurture these plants she would periodically open the windows of heaven and pour water upon the ground. She created humans and other animals to eat the food and fruits produced by the plants. In those days, all the animals were able to talk and communicate with each other.

Time went by and the creatures reproduced and multiplied. They co-existed in harmony, never harmed each other, and never lacked for food. Still, as the population increased, animals of different natures and temperaments emerged, and they decided that they needed a ruler to protect and rule over them.

So they chose one among them to be their king. His name was Hauhulh, and he was from the Pawi clan. He travelled to the West, to Sialsuk, and there he established a village.

The Swallowing of the Moon

One night, after having had his supper, King Hauhulh took a nap. It was the night of the full moon, and all the creatures were making merry, dancing and singing and celebrating in the moonlight. But in the midst of their revelry, the moonlight suddenly began to fade. They all looked up and were shocked to see the moon disappearing even as they watched. Frantic with worry, the creatures decided they should make as much noise as possible to scare away whatever it was that was eating the moon. They grabbed whatever objects they could find that would produce sound and started banging on them as hard as they could, creating a cacophonous din. Soon, to their great relief, the moon reappeared.

The tremendous noise that his subjects had made woke the king from his sleep. He asked the elders what had happened, and they told him. The king said, "Listen: while I was asleep, I dreamt that I had swallowed the moon. Afterwards I heard a terrific noise, and I got so scared that I spat the moon back out again—though it was very difficult to do!" The elders then noticed that there were deep gashes and bloodstains at the corners of the king's mouth, and they believed that it was true: the king really had swallowed the moon.

Thimzing, the Great Darkness

Not long afterwards, King Hauhulh died. He went to Piarlal, as the Mizos call Heaven, where he was transformed into a creature called the Awk, who could—and often did—swallow the moon.

The Awk could swallow the sun, as well, causing eclipses. Once, it swallowed the sun for such a long time that the whole earth was plunged into total darkness for a whole day and night. There was complete chaos. Nobody could see anything, and nobody could do any work. This time of darkness was called the Thimzing.

During the Thimzing, many sudden and mysterious transformations began to occur. Some humans became monkeys, while others became gibbons. Some of the young boys and girls were transformed into koro birds (white-crested laughing thrushes, as they are called in English). A group of people who had lit torches so they could see in the darkness were transformed into fireflies. The most famous wrestlers of the village were all turned into bears. Most of the members of the Vangchhia clan were transformed into elephants, while the members of the Paite and Vuite clans became squirrels. The village elders became vakul birds (drongos, as they are called in English), and those men who were renowned as hunters were turned into tigers.

It wasn't just the humans. The domestic animals began to be transformed into wild birds and beasts, as well.

Chhinlung

The goddess Khuazingnu, who had made the humans, saw her creations being changed into lesser beings, and she became very distressed. Before they could all be transformed, she decided to take a couple from each human clan, as well as a representative couple of each animal species, and place them inside a deep cave.

Once the couples were all inside, she sealed the cave with a huge rock called Chhinlung.

After four or five generations had been born inside the cave, Khuazingnu decided that there were enough people to repopulate the earth. Gingerly, she lifted the rock Chhinlung. She heard a loud buzzing sound from within. When she opened the covering fully, humans swarmed out from behind the rock in great multitudes, the way termites emerge from their hole during the rainy season. All the different clans were there: the Hmar, the Chawte, the Ngente, the Pantu, the Lushai, and more. Then the Ralte clan emerged in great numbers—noisier than the other clans, and full of arrogance. At this point, the goddess decided that there were enough people in the world, and she placed Chhinlung back over the mouth of the cave.

The Feast of Thlanrawkpa

While they had been sealed off from the world under the great rock Chhinlung, the humans had cohabited freely with supernatural creatures called the Lasi, who were like elves or faeries, and could make themselves invisible. They had even produced offspring with them. These half-human half-Lasi children tended to be bigger and stronger than normal people.

Among those children born of liaisons between humans and Lasi was a boy named Thlanrawkpa.

Thlanrawkpa soon grew into a tall, powerful man. He was big and strong even compared to the other half-Lasi. He was the first man to domesticate the sial—that is, the Indian bison, also known as the gaur or mithun. As a result of this accomplishment, his people elected him to be their chief.

Thlanrawkpa was also renowned as a hunter, and he became very rich. As befitted a man of his accomplishments and stature, he decided to host the ceremony known as Khuangchawi. On the eve of the ceremony, a tall pillar would be planted in the ground. A sial would be killed, and its large horned head would be fixed to the top of the pillar. The next day the whole community would be treated to a sumptuous feast, with plenty of meat and rice beer. By these means Thlanrawkpa would secure easy passage for himself and his relations to the heavenly realm of Pialral after death. Furthermore, Thlankrawkpa planned to get married at the ceremony, to the daughter of a god named Sabereka.

Unfortunately, Thlanrawkpa forgot to invite Sabereka, his father-in-law-to-be, to the function. Sabereka was furious at being slighted. He called down a thunderstorm on the eve of the feast, and it rained the entire night. The rain was so heavy that it washed away all the houses. (Before Sabereka's thunderstorm, people used to build their houses on the ground, with mud floors. Ever since that torrential rain Mizos have built their houses on stilts, to avoid such calamities.)

The rain kept pouring down until it had washed away all the soil in the village. By morning, when it finally stopped, the bedrock beneath lay exposed. There was no way anyone could farm or grow food. Not only that; there was no way the villagers could dig a hole into the hard rock to mount the pillar for the sial's head. And without this, the Khuangchawi could not take place.

Some distance from the village there was a wide river called Tuihuanghriam. Across the water, on the other side of the river, was a fertile expanse of earth that had not been affected by the rains. But the waters of Tuihuanghriam were very dangerous; whoever had tried to cross it in the past had perished.

The Otter and the Badger, who had thick waterproof fur coats, bravely volunteered to make trips across the water to bring soil to their village. Back and forth and back and forth they swam, until they had brought back a great deal of soil. Then the Earthworm volunteered to eat it, so that the dirt would be aerated and its volume multiplied once he excreted it.

The legendary Chhurbura was there too; he offered to beat the earth with a huge mallet to make it flat. While he was doing this, his mallet head flew off the handle, and landed miles away. (Beside the path between the villages of Leng and Lingvum, five miles from Vanlaiphai Valley, there is a large cylindrical stone, and some say that this is Chhurbura's lost mallet head.)

In this way, all the creatures of the village cooperated with one another, contributing to the community work until the earth became habitable again, and the glorious feast could finally be held.

The Naming of the Animals

In those days many of the animals did not have names. As the guests came one by one to attend the Khuangchawi, Thlanrawkpa gave them names according to the manner of their arrival, or the tricks they performed. For example, the hen arrived by splashing up through a large puddle of mud, so Thlanrawkpa named her Chirhi, which means mud; and that is why Mizos call *chiri chiri* to their hens today. One of the last guests to arrive was the rat; she was late because she had spent a long time brewing rice beer for the feast. Since "zu" means rice beer and "rei" means long, she was named Zuhrei—slow beer.

Later on there were competitions. The first competition was to see who had the best balance. The cat showed how it could walk across a thin bamboo pole, and so it was named Zawhte, which means "narrow walk". Next was the squirrel, which walked across a rope that was even thinner than the bamboo. It was named Theihlei, which means "even more agile", and was awarded the first prize: the rights to eat ripe fruit from all the trees. The cat got the second prize: the right to curl up next to the fireplace, and to bury its droppings in the ash.

No other animal could balance very well, and so the third prize went unclaimed.

Having given all the creatures names, Thlanrawkpa encouraged them to make friends with one other, which they did. They stayed up late into the night, practicing their dance moves.

The Bamboo Rat and the Drum

Some of the animals, like the Earthworm and the Owl, had told Thlanrawkpa that they could not dance when the sun was out, as they would die from the heat. So Thlanrawkpa had requested the sun to stay behind the clouds all the next day.

The merry-making continued. The music was provided by the Buipui—the Bamboo Rat—who played the traditional drum called a khuang. Everyone was dancing. The mood was so festive that when someone stuck some feathers into a pile of pig dung, even the pig dung started to dance!

Meanwhile, Zuhrei, the big rat, had put some feathers in her hair too. When she danced the other creatures thought she was very beautiful. They sang:

"Watch the Zuhrei with feathers in her hair,
What beauty, what grace she has!"

The Bamboo Rat, who was watching all this while he played his khuang, became jealous. He plucked some flowers and put them in his hair, and began to dance himself. But this only made him look ridiculous, and the other creatures jeered:

"Watch the Buipui with flowers in his hair,
No beauty, no grace at all!"

This made the Buipui so angry that he took his khuang, stormed off, and crawled deep into his burrow. Since the party couldn't proceed without the drum, the other animals tried as hard as they could to cajole him out of his hole, but he would not be mollified.

Eventually someone got the idea of pouring water down one end of the burrow. The Buipui emerged from the other end, dripping wet and still sulking, and threw out the khuang. The hen was standing nearby, and the drum hit her in the knee joints. To this day, the hen's knee joints are bent backwards as a result.

The Loris and the Sun

Once they had the drum back, the revellers resumed their merry-making. This time, it was Sahuai—the Slow Loris—who led the dance.

But while they were dancing, the sun—who had grown very impatient from waiting, and was anxious to get a glimpse of the festivities—began to peek through the clouds. As soon as it appeared, the Sahuai tried to stop it from coming up. He knew that if the sun shone too bright, the Earthworm and the Owl would not be able to dance anymore, and the pile of pig dung would dry up and not be able to move.

So the Sahuai tried and tried; but the sun could not be held back for long. Soon it broke though the clouds, and before long the pig dung dried up and stopped moving, and then all the animals got tired, and the dancing stopped.

The Sahuai was so angry that he vowed eternal war against the sun. And to this day, the Loris refuses to look up. If you turn its head towards the sky, you will find that its eyes will always be closed.

The Tortoise and the Python's Eggs

The festivities stretched on for many days, and at one point, the Python needed to leave her nest. She asked the tortoise to do her the favour of watching over her eggs. The Tortoise agreed, but soon after the Python left, a group of animals gathered around and began a jumping contest.

"Come on," said the Barking Deer to the Tortoise, "let's jump over the Python's nest."

"I don't think I can do that," said the Tortoise. "And if I break her eggs, the Python will kill me!"

"Oh don't worry," said the Deer. "I'll protect you in case you break something."

So the Tortoise agreed to the contest.

The Deer went first. He got a good running start and easily cleared the nest. But when it was the Tortoise's turn, he was so slow and heavy that he landed on the eggs with a splat, and crushed them all.

"You'd better run away," the Deer.

"But you said you would protect me!" protested the Tortoise.

"Sorry," said the Deer, "but actually I'm terribly afraid of the Python. I can't help you."

And so the Tortoise ran away as fast as he could—which was not very fast. On his way he tripped and tumbled into a bear's hollow.

"Who's there?" shouted the bear.

"It's me, Tortoise," said the Tortoise.

"Why are you running? What are you so afraid of?" asked the bear.

"It's the Python," said the Tortoise, "I broke her eggs, and now I'm very afraid. Please help me."

"Sorry," said the bear, "but I'm terribly afraid of the Python. I can't help you."

The Tortoise went everywhere looking for protection. He went to the tiger, the wild boar, the stag, and the wild goat, but all of them were too afraid of the Python to offer their help. Finally he came to the tree where the Mura lived.

(The Mura was a fearsome predatory bird that lived in those days—like a gigantic eagle, but so huge that it hunted human children, and sometimes even adults. It had a cruel tactic: it would perch on the roof of a hut and push its giant tail in through the back door. The people inside would try and escape through the front door, at which point the Mura would snap them up and eat them. There is a cave in Zote Village, near Champhai, called Mura Puk, where it is said that the local people used to hide from the Mura.)

"Who's there?" asked the Mura.

"It's me, Tortoise," said the Tortoise.

"What do you want?" said the Mura.

"The Deer and I were having a jumping contest," said the Tortoise. "I tried to jump over the Python's nest and I broke all her eggs. I'm terribly afraid of the Python and no one will help me. I came to you hoping for your protection."

"Don't worry," said the Mura. "I'll help you."

In the meantime, the Python had discovered that her eggs had been smashed, and of course she was furious. She had been searching everywhere for the Tortoise, and finally she found his footprints. Hissing with rage, she followed them to the tree where the Mura was nesting.

"What's that dreadful noise?" asked the Mura.

"It's the Python!" answered the Tortoise. "What should I do now?"

"Hide under my wing," said the Mura.

When the Python reached the base of the Mura's tree, she asked, "Have you seen the Tortoise?"

"No, I haven't," said the Mura.

The Python had followed the Tortoise's clear trail of footprints right up to the base of this tree, so she didn't believe the Mura. "Spread your wings and let me see," she said.

The Mura spread one of its wings, to show that there was nothing there.

"Spread the other one, too," said the Python.

"I'm sorry, but I can't spread the other one," said the Mura. "It's sore, and it hurts terribly if I stretch it out."

"Open it a little bit, then," demanded the Python. The Mura spread his other wing a little bit, and though he tried his best to conceal him under the rest of his wing, the Tortoise's tail was visible, and the Python spied it at once.

The Python was angry with the Tortoise, but she was even more furious with the Mura for lying to her. At that moment, she declared war: a war between the animals that walked and crawled and slithered on the land on one side, and the animals that lived in the trees and flew through the air on the other.

The Great War of Animals

Quickly the two armies assembled: the land animals, led by the Python, and the flying animals, led by the Mura.

The army of birds was perched on a branch of a huge banyan tree, busily planning their strategy of attack. Suddenly the Python lifted herself high into the air and brought her heavy body down on the branch, smashing it to pieces and scattering the birds. The land animals cheered and jumped with joy.

After some time, the birds all settled on another branch of the same tree. Again the Python lifted herself up and smashed the branch, bringing it down with a great crash!

Things were not looking good at this point for the flying creatures. The Bat, who had been with the birds' army, felt sure that the land animals were going to win the war. I should switch sides! he thought. So he flew down to the army on the ground. "Look at me!" he cried, "Look at my head and teeth. I should be on your side." And so the Bat joined the army of the land animals.

The war raged on. The smallest of the land animals fought with the smallest tree-dwellers, and the largest beasts fought the largest birds. The battle was very fierce.

After some time, there was a lull, and the birds gathered again on yet another branch. Once again, the Python raised herself up in an attempt to break it, but this time the branch was too strong: she merely hung there, her body draped over the tree.

The Mura saw his chance. He swooped down and bit through the Python's spine, killing her at once. Now it was the turn of the flying creatures to cheer and jump for joy!

Seeing this, the Bat grew nervous. Perhaps I made a mistake, he thought. I should be with the flying creatures! And he flew up to the army in the trees. "Look at me!" he cried, "Look at my wings! I should be on your side." And so the Bat changed armies again.

Human beings are land creatures too, and they joined the fighting. The Mura began hunting them whenever it could.

At one point the Mura captured two humans whose nicknames were Chera and Thauva. Chera means "thin" in Mizo, and Thauva means "fat"; and as you might guess, Chera was very lean and Thauva was very stout. The Mura had to think for a moment. "Should I eat the thin one or the fat one?" he muttered to himself.

Chera, whose real name was Mualbeuva, overheard this, and he said to the Mura: "You should eat Thauva first; he will make a better meal."

The Mura was easily convinced, and began eating Thauva. But Thauva was so fat that it took the Mura three consecutive days to finish eating him, and by the time he was done he was completely full and very drowsy. Once the Mura was incapacitated, Mualbeuva took out the knife he'd been hiding under his clothes, crept up on the Mura, and stabbed him to death.

And so, with the death of the Mura, the war was finally won for the land animals. They decided that they would celebrate their victory, and that this celebration would mark the culmination of the great feast hosted by Thlanrawkpa.

As the earth-bound creatures celebrated, the domesticated animals began making demands for greater respect. They refused to bow down to the dictates of their human masters any longer, claiming that they should have a more exalted position because of their contributions to the victory. They raised a great protest when some of them were to be slaughtered for the feast.

Finally, Thlanrawkpa's wife had to call on her father, the god Sabereka, to intervene. Sabereka decreed that from then on the animals and humans would no longer be able to speak the same language.

With communication thus cut off, the creatures could no longer make protests. Order was restored, with humans prevailing as masters over other living things. The earth-bound creatures and the flying creatures no longer fought each other.

But the cowardly Bat, who kept changing allegiances during the conflict, could not show his face to either side. He had to go live in a cave, and could only ever come out at night!

The Story of Tlingi & Ngama

Once upon a time there were two women who would help each other out when they worked in their fields, as was the custom in those days. These two women both had infant children. One had a son, whose name was Ngambawma, or Ngama for short. The other woman had a daughter, whose name was Zawltlingi, or Tlingi for short.

Every day, the two women would take their infants to the fields; and, since the babies were not old enough to crawl or move on their own, the mothers would leave them in the shelter hut. They would set them down far apart from each other, while they went off to do the hard work of weeding and cultivating the fields.

In the mornings, Ngama's mother usually left the shelter later than Tlingi's mother. As she went out, she would put her son down near the doorway of the shelter, while Tlingi lay farther inside. However, whenever the two women returned to the shelter for their midday meal or at the end of the working day, they would find the babies sleeping serenely close together. This caused them much amazement. "Mother of Ngama," Tlingi's mother said, "you say that you leave our babies to sleep separately since you are the last to leave the shelter; and yet they are always sleeping together when we return. Are you actually making them lie next to each other?"

To this, Ngama's mother only replied, "Mother of Tlingi, perhaps tomorrow you should leave the shelter after me, and see what happens for yourself."

The next morning, as they had discussed, Ngama's mother left first, and Tlingi's mother left second. As she left the babies, she placed Ngama near the entrance of the shelter and her own daughter towards the back of the shelter, in their usual places, far apart from each other. As noon approached and it came time for the midday meal, both women returned to the shelter and found their babies sleeping peacefully together again, as always. This filled the women with wonder, for neither child had been seen to crawl yet. They could not understand how it happened.

As time went by, the two babies became beautiful children whose affection and friendship kept growing stronger. By the time they became young adults, they had eyes for only each other. When they came of marriageable age, Ngama quite predictably sent emissaries to Tlingi's parents to propose marriage. However, quite unexpectedly, Tlingi's mother refused to give consent to their marriage, and the proposal was rejected. The emissaries could not make her change her mind, and they returned crestfallen, having given up on their mission.

However, the rejection of the proposal did nothing to affect the love that Tlingi and Ngama had for each other. In fact, it strengthened their bond even more, and they eventually found themselves having a physical relationship. They knew that this would be frowned upon, and they decided to run away rather than risk the wrath of their elders. They picked a day to run away and planned to meet at a certain hillock at the crack of dawn, near a massive termite mound. Tlingi reached first and hid from sight on one side of the termite mound, so that nobody would notice her. When Ngama arrived next, he hid on the other side of the termite mound, staying quiet so that nobody would notice him. The two of them waited for each other like that for a long time, scared to call out or make any noise to draw attention, and because they were each hiding on opposite sides of the mound, they could not see each other.

A long time went by, until Tlingi finally gave up waiting. "He must have gone on ahead without me," she thought. Taking the bamboo stick she had with her, she firmly thrust it into the spot where she had been waiting, and there it later took root. Similarly, Ngama, who had been silently waiting for a long time, eventually gave up waiting for his beloved too. He also planted the bamboo stick he held into the ground, and it too took root. To this day, in the east, they say those bamboo groves flourish still.

Though the two lovers had given up waiting for each other at the ant-hill, they each decided to make their own way to their planned destination. Fortunately, since they were headed in the same direction, it was just a matter of time before their paths crossed and they were ecstatically reunited.

When news of their elopement became known, the entire village came together and searched high and low for the errant pair, but had no luck in finding them. There was no way of knowing if the two young lovers were dead or alive, if they were hiding nearby, or if they had run far away to a land beyond the horizon. Eventually the villagers lost all hope of ever seeing Tlingi and Ngama alive again.

As they started their new life together, Tlingi and Ngama made a dwelling for themselves in a cave in the forest. Since they had left home a long time ago, their clothing had become ragged and tattered. They had to fashion coverings for themselves out of Hnahthial leaves, but they were content. Ngama would often lyrically say:

"Tlingi and Ngama are not forlorn;
with beautiful leaves they themselves adorn."

Time went by and they eventually had a child. Since they lived in a cave near a cliff, there was a perilous drop near their dwelling, and their lively little child loved crawling right up to the edge. Whenever the child got too close to the cliffs, Tlingi and Ngama would get his attention by beating softly on a small gourd, so as to warn him to come back without startling him. One day, as a group of hunters passed by the cave, they heard the soft thumps of Tlingi and Ngama hitting the gourd to warn their baby. The hunters followed the sound and spotted the little family living in the cave. When these men returned home to the village, they conveyed what they discovered in the forest, and the parents of both Tlingi and Ngama sent emissaries to their children, begging them to come back and have a normal married life at home. Comforted by this warm message, Tlingi and Ngama decided to return to their village with their baby, where they proceeded to set up and enjoy the comforts of home, a far cry from their rough life in the forest.

But they could not enjoy this new life for long. Tlingi suddenly fell ill and died shortly after. Ngama mourned his loss so deeply that he did not know what to do with himself. Every morning he visited Tlingi's grave, where he had carefully planted beautiful cockscomb flowers. (The Mizo traditionally believe that cockscomb dazzles the eyes of evil spirits, so that they cannot see any humans standing near the plants; this makes them a popular flower to plant by homes and graves alike.)

After a while, on his morning visits, Ngama began to notice that the cockscomb flowers looked like they had been plucked and torn during the night. Furious, he decided to catch the disrespectful vandals in the act. Early one morning, well before daybreak, he hid by the grave and lay in wait for the miscreants.

As dawn neared, a couple of martens edged near the grave. The small, weasel-like creatures plucked some of the beautiful flowers. Filled with rage, Ngama pounced upon them and grabbed them, shouting, "So, you two have been plucking the flowers from my wife's grave! How dare you! I shall kill you!" The martens struggled and pleaded with him to let them go. But Ngama replied, "No, I will not let you go, I am going to kill you!" The martens protested,

"We are not stealing your flowers of our own will, we are simply doing as our mistress Tlingi wishes!"

As soon as Ngama heard the name of his departed wife, he froze in amazement. "Did you say Tlingi sent you? Is that true?" he asked.

They replied, "Yes, it is true. She insists on having only these flowers and sends us to fetch them."

Ngama said, "I am her husband, Ngama, and I must see her again. I will follow you when you return to her."

The martens tried to dissuade him. "Master," they warned, "you will not be able to undertake the journey. The way is dangerous; we must go over steep cliffs and perilous rocky paths. You will not make it."

But Ngama remained steadfast. "In that case," he said, "I will hold on to your tails."

At last, the martens were convinced, and off the three of them went, Ngama holding fast to the tails of the martens as they traversed the cliffs and rocks and all manner of dangerous terrain.

At long last, they reached their destination, the Land of the Dead. When they reached the outskirts of the village, they saw that several dead people were struggling to split something in sections. It was a Telhawng plant—a wild plant with a woody stem that has snake-like markings.

"What are you doing that for?" Ngama asked the dead people, approaching them with curiosity.

They answered, "It is for the floor of our mistress Tlingi's house."

As soon as he heard this, Ngama offered, "Here, let me do it," and easily split the stem into sections with his bare hands.

Later, Ngama found his way to Tlingi's abode and the two lovers finally met again for the first time since her death. When they saw each other, they were overjoyed. But things were not as they had been before; life was drastically different here in the Land of the Dead. Tlingi, who once was a beautiful, rosy-cheeked girl, had become thin and pale. When they lay down to sleep at night, Tlingi would lie upside-down on the bed.

Ngama witnessed many strange things in the Land of the Dead. One morning, he heard a commotion outside – judging by their shouts, the dead people seemed to be trying to catch a bear.

"There he goes, towards that Human Ngama, he's trying to escape!" they shouted.

Ngama, confused, asked, "Where is it?" looking around in bewilderment. There was no bear in sight, just a caterpillar crawling in his direction. Suddenly, he had a realization. Stepping forward, he asked, "Is this what you are trying to capture?" As he lowered his foot, he stepped on the caterpillar and squashed it to death.

The Dead cried out in excitement, "The Human Ngama has felled a bear!" Delighted, they proceeded to cut the caterpillar's head off, and then they mounted it on a stack and displayed it as a trophy above Tlingi's door.

Another time, the entire community of the Dead went fishing, and Ngama too decided to join in. When they reached the river, which was full of dry leaves, the Dead cried out in excitement "Fish!" and tried to grab as many leaves as they could. Ngama, following suit, scooped up great handfuls of dead leaves with his hands. The Dead exulted, "Human Ngama is the best fisherman!"

By then it was getting dark, and they all decided to head home. As the hero of the day, they asked Ngama to decide how they would get home: should they go by *khup suk* or *thopa zuan*?

Now *khup suk* means to move the knees up and down; but metaphorically, it also means to make no progress, to be indolent, to keep taking breaks in one's work. *Thopa zuan* is the term for the way a male fly moves.

Ngama had no idea what they were talking about. He bemusedly said, "How about thopa zuan?" to which the Dead said, "Alright!" and immediately disappeared into thin air.

This left poor Ngama all by himself in the dark wilderness, trying to find his way home.

When his fellow fishermen arrived home, Tlingi was quick to ask, "Where is Ngama?" The dead fishermen explained that Ngama had chosen thopa zuan as his preferred way of going home, so that was how they had all returned. Tlingi immediately chastised them, saying, "Ngama doesn't understand what that means! He must be lost in the wild. You must go back and lead him home!"

So the Dead turned themselves into fireflies and went to lead Ngama home. By the light they provided, Ngama somehow managed to find his way back.

When he reached home Tlingi said, "It is unfortunate that your friends left you to get home on your own. I scolded them and sent them back to lead you home."

Ngama, of course, had no idea that the fireflies had come there specially to escort him home. He replied, "Nobody came to rescue me, I got home by myself." Tlingi, concerned, asked him, "Wait, Ngama, did you not see anything or anyone helping you?" to which he shook his head. "Not a thing," he replied, "except many fireflies flying around me."

"Ah," Tlingi explained, "Those were no ordinary fireflies! Those were our friends, who came to help rescue you using thopa zuan." Bemused, Ngama replied, "I see. I did wonder why there were so many fireflies around me on my way home!"

Tlingi then asked Ngama, "Well, how did your fishing trip go? Did you catch a lot of fish?" to which Ngama disconsolately replied, "Not at all! Check my bag and you will see!" As far as he knew, all he had in his bag was dried leaves. But when Tlingi examined his bag she exclaimed, "My goodness! That is quite a catch! So many fish and such big ones too! Who could ask for more?" For what Ngama saw as dead leaves, Tlingi saw as the choicest fish. Together they roasted the fish-leaves over the fire. Whatever Tlingi roasted looked appetizing and savory, but when Ngama tried roasting the leaves, they simply dried up and burned until finally Tlingi said in exasperation, "Stop roasting the fish, you are too wasteful. At that rate we will have nothing left to eat!"

Sadly, happenings like these took their toll. One day, Tlingi finally said, "Ngama, no matter how much we miss each other, it is impossible for us to live together now, because we are too different. Go back home to the land of the living and live a good life. Harvest as much food as you can and when your harvest is ready, leave aside some for me as an offering. As you have seen, here in the Land of the Dead, we have barely enough to eat, and we grow thin and weak." At these words, Ngama, who had actually been in a trance-like state for the entire time he'd spent in the Land of the Dead, suddenly woke up and found himself back in the Land of the Living. He was filled with loneliness and missed his wife more than ever.

He remembered what Tlingi had requested of him and quickly went towards his fields to look for freshly grown vegetables for her. There, he gathered the best produce of his land, filling his basket to the brim before heading back. When he reached home, just as he was about to cross over the threshold, he was struck by the thought that there was nobody to greet him or receive his harvest. Enveloped with despair, he fell to the ground in a panic, spilling the contents of his basket with the choicest produce all over the floor. Weakly, he muttered, "Tlingi, I have gathered these for you. Please eat them." And as he lost consciousness he became possessed once more by the spirit of the Dead, and found himself back in the Land of the Dead.

When he saw his beloved Tlingi again, he was surprised to see that she now looked plump, healthy, and beautiful. He asked in confusion, "Tlingi, when I saw you a few days ago, you were thin and weak and sallow. How are you this radiant and beautiful now?" to which she replied, "I have been eating all the food that you sacrificed for me. How could I not thrive?"

As they entered her house, Ngama noticed that her floorboards and her bed were all made of beautiful wood. Ngama asked her how this transformation had happened to her house. Tlingi explained, "These are the Telhawng wood planks you made for me on your last visit." Then he asked about the bear's head trophy hanging above her doorway, and she said, "That is the bear you killed on your last visit here."

When they sat down to eat dinner, Tlingi brought out a heaping plate of preserved dried fish. Ngama exclaimed, "Eheu! How do you have so much fish?!" to which she replied, to Ngama's amazement, "Oh, this is the fish you caught on your last visit here; this time, you are able to see everything that you could not see on your last visit!"

However, since Ngama was only possessed by the spirit of the Dead and not really dead, he once again woke up from his stupor to his own reality, forlorn and lonely. For the rest of his life, he was never again able to visit the Land of the Dead. But every year from then on, during harvest season, he dedicated a portion of his choicest harvest for his dead wife Tlingi. People became curious as to why Ngama would always keep an untouched heap of the finest vegetables in a designated part of his house, and asked him why he did it.

"Ah," Ngama would say, "let me tell you a story." And he would speak in great detail of the Land of the Dead, and of how, after he had dedicated a portion of his harvest to Tlingi after his first visit, she was thriving and blooming the next time he saw her. People who heard his story and who had lost loved ones of their own felt that they ought to do the same for their dead, to help them thrive in the Land of the Dead. Soon it became a widespread tradition among the Mizo people, and legend has it that this is how the practice of setting aside a portion of the harvest for dead family members during the festival of Mim Kut began.

Chhura & the Ai-Um

Once when Chhura was away visiting some friends, they served him a delicious meal with ai-um, a fermented crab delicacy that he had never tasted before. He loved the dish so much that he was determined to get the recipe and ask his wife to make it for him when he returned from his travels. He eagerly asked his hosts, "What is this delicious item that you have served me?"

"It is ai-um," the hostess replied.

Shortly after, he thanked his hosts and departed on his way home.

Chhura was worried that he would forget the name of the dish that had won his heart so completely, and on his way home he kept repeating to himself "Ai-um, ai-um, ai-um." Unfortunately, he suddenly lost his footing on a slippery patch of clay and landed on his bottom. This unexpected turn of events caught him so completely by surprise that he forgot the word that he had been saying over and over again. He got up from the ground, dusted himself off, and looked all around the spot where he had fallen, searching for the lost word. Down on his knees, he cleared away the fallen leaves, the twigs, and the pebbles with his hands, scrabbling through the slippery clay, but he could not find his lost word.

Just then a Pawi man, no doubt on his way to a faraway destination, chanced upon him. Chhura saw him and instantly appealed,

"Hey you, Pawi, can you help me look for this thing that I have lost?"

The Pawi man agreed to help him and asked, "What is it that you have lost?"

Chhura replied, "If I knew what it was, I would not need your help to look for it."

And so the two of them looked around earnestly for the thing that was lost. Finally, the Pawi man somewhat exasperatedly exclaimed, "You don't even know what we are looking for; and here you are, reeking of ai-um!"

At that instant, Chhura ecstatically shouted, "Yes! That is it! That is what I have been looking for! I lost the word!" and happily proceeded home, once more chanting "Ai-um, ai-um, ai-um."

The Story of Sichangneii

Once there was a widower who would go early every morning to fetch water from a pond. Although he went at the crack of dawn, there seemed to be somebody who went even earlier than him, because the water was always muddy. He wondered who it could be that disturbed the water so early in the morning every time.

One day, an old lady who lived nearby said to him, "I know who muddies the water. It is the lovely Sichangneii and her sister. They fly down from the skies every morning to bathe in the water, and that is why the water is disturbed. If you can capture one of them, you could make her your wife, for they are beautiful, and you would be a lucky man indeed! However, if you mean to catch them, you must sneak up on them from behind, otherwise their loveliness will dazzle you and you will not be able to capture either of them."

The following morning, at the first crow of the rooster, the man was already lying in wait for the sisters, hidden from view. Just as the old lady had said, Sichangneii and her sisters flew down from the sky to bathe. They were so lovely that rays of light emanated from them. On their backs were attached beautiful wings with lustrous feathers. Seeing them, the man dove towards them in a great rush, trying to capture one of the lovely beings, but alas! He missed and landed with a thud on the ground. At this, the sisters quickly flew up to the sky and eluded him.

The next morning, more determined than ever, the man set out and waited for the sisters again. He managed to capture the older of the sisters, Sichangneii. He took her home, where he removed her feathers and cut off her wings, and hid them inside the hollow of a large container fashioned out of bamboo. Then he stored the bamboo container on the upper shelf above the fireplace.

And so, the two of them were married.

As time went on, they were blessed with seven healthy and strong sons. Their names were Kaptheia, which means "Good Shooter"; Dotheia, which means "Able to Prop Heavy Things Up"; Entheia, which means "Sharp Eyes"; Haitheia, which means "Clearer and Digger"; Chhintheia, which means "Good at Covering Things"; Mantheia, which means "Catcher"; and the last was called Tlumtea, which means "Youngest".

The man and his wife worked every day in their field. Since they had many sons who were born close together, both of them could not go to the field at the same time; one of them had to take care of their children at home.

On the days when it was the father's turn to babysit at home, he would take down his wife's wings from the shelf and let the boys play with them. The boys would stick the feathers on themselves and dance around with glee, and they always had great fun. But when it was Sichangneii's turn to babysit them, she did not anything fun with them, and the boys would be bored.

One day, when the mother was at home with her boys, the youngest, Tlumtea, said, "Mother, when Father babysits us, he takes out feathers with which we adorn ourselves, and we dance merrily and always have a great time."

Now the father had always told his sons, "Never tell your Mother about the feathers," and up until then none of the brothers had ever revealed the secret. So when Tlumtea blurted it out to their mother, the others said, "Silly boy! He is lying!"

But their mother persisted. "Tlumte, where does your father keep those feathers?" And Tlumtea replied, "Inside the bamboo container on the upper shelf above the fireplace."

His mother said, "Go and fetch it," and Tlumtea went to fetch it. The mother excitedly took out her feathers and her wings and put them on. She stepped outside, preening herself, and asked, "Children, do I look nice?"

The oldest son replied, "No you don't. I am ashamed of you. People might see you. Come inside!" and five of his younger brothers agreed. However, Tlumtea said, "Mother, you look beautiful and lovely."

She then gracefully hopped on to the overhead railing on the platform built at the side of the house and asked again, "Children, do I look nice?" All her sons gave her the same reply except Tlumtea, who insisted, "Mother, you look beautiful!"

Then their mother flapped her wings and flew up towards her home in the sky.

Evening came, and the Father got home from the fields. "Where is your mother?" he asked, and his sons told him all that had happened.

When he heard this, the man was filled with despair. He said, "Since your mother is gone, I shall kill myself by crushing my testicles." His sons begged him not to do so, all except silly little Tlumtea, who said, "Go ahead Father, why don't you do it?" and so his father crushed one of his testicles with a mallet. Then he said, "Let me also crush the other one," and his sons replied once more, "Father, do not do it, we beg you!" But Tlumtea, eager and curious to see what would happen, said, "Yes Father, you should crush the other one as well."

So their father went ahead and crushed the other side. As he thrashed around on the floor in agony, writhing in the throes of death, Tlumtea excitedly cried, "Look! Father is dancing!" and started banging the empty bamboo cups on the floor in rhythm with his father's convulsions.

The father soon died, and they were left all alone.

Lost and forlorn, they did not know what to do. Finally, they said, "Enthei, can you try and see where our mother is?" So Entheia trained his sharp eyes on the horizon and upwards, and finally saw his mother pounding rice in the sky. At this, Kaptheia shot an arrow that landed right on the edge of their mother's mortar where she was pounding rice. Their mother looked down and saw them and she threw down a rope for them to climb up.

At their mother's house, there also lived a cannibal who hated the brothers. They were required to work in the fields with this cannibal every day. The cannibal wanted to kill the brothers, and he devised a plan to make a large tree fall upon them. One day, he secretly cut the tree with an axe, to the point where it was nearly ready to fall. When the time for the mid-day meal came, he brought all of them under the tree that was ready to fall, and made them eat there. As they were starting their meal, the cannibal said, "Carry on with your meal. I need to go and do something over there," and left them. Then he went and used his axe to fell the tree. The mighty tree slowly started to descend upon the alarmed brothers. At this, they said, "Dothei, prop that tree up!" and Dotheia propped the tree up. Then Haitheia cleared the tree away. When the cannibal returned, he said, "Ho! I thought you would all be dead," and they replied, "We have no intention of dying, you dirty, treacherous scum!"

Some time later, the cannibal took the brothers to burn the jhum fields, which is a common practice to get rid of tree stumps and unwanted debris. He left them in the part of the field where there were piles of bamboos, trees, and other jungle debris ready for burning. Then he said, "Wait here for me and eat your meal while I go to the bottom of the field and try to catch some crabs at the stream. Don't go anywhere until I return." And he left them alone.

As soon as he reached the bottom of the field, he lit a fire which rapidly burned towards the place where the brothers sat waiting. As soon as they saw the fire, they were alarmed. They shouted,

"Haithei, clear the way! Clear the way!" Haitheia quickly cleared all the debris. Then he dug a hole into which they all went and Chhintheia covered the opening of the hole. When the fire had died down, the cannibal returned to the place where he had left the brothers. There he found the remains of a termite mound. When he saw the charred, ash-white shapes of the towers, he said, "These must be the remains of their skulls," and picked them up and popped them happily into his mouth.

A little while later, however, the brothers emerged from their hole, and the cannibal saw them unharmed and safe. Flustered, he blurted out, "You are still safe? I thought you had all burned to ashes!" and they replied, "We have no intention of being burned, you ugly scoundrel!"

When they reached home, they related all that had happened to their mother. Their mother, worried, said, "This man is a cannibal. If you remain here, he will surely one day succeed in killing you. The safest thing for you to do is to go away from here and return to Earth. When you reach there, set your traps on Seventh Mound."

Obeying their mother, they all left to go back to Earth. On their return to Earth, they did as their mother had directed and set traps on Seventh Mound, which proved very lucky for them. They caught all kinds of game; sometimes their bamboo baskets would be bursting with the dozens of animals they had managed to trap. One afternoon, after a successful day of trapping, the brothers all sat together on the house platform, enjoying their feast of meat that they had caught. Arrogantly, they said, "Here we are, enjoying such bounties! We can have all this food to ourselves; our parents have abandoned us, so there shall be no share for them!"

Just at that moment, their mother, who had been husking grain up in the sky, dumped the husks and chaff of the grain onto the brothers, blinding them.

Although blind, the brothers continued to go to Seventh Mound to collect the animals that had been trapped there. Whenever they collected their game, they would distribute it equally among themselves. Now it so happened that a Chawmnu—a big, burly, hairy, female evil spirit—would secretly hold out her hands for a share without the brothers knowing. And she always got some part. After a while, the brothers began to realize that they each seemed to get slightly less than the correct portion of what they had caught.

One day Tlumtea said, "Let me be the one to distribute the catch," and so he started handing out the meat. But before he gave out each portion, he held the outstretched hand of each person and asked, "Whose hand is this?" The brothers identified themselves one after the other, saying "Mine", and Tlumtea recognized each of their voices, and gave each their share. When he felt the seventh outstretched hand, he asked once again, "Whose hand is this?" But nobody said, "Mine."

Knowing something was wrong, Tlumtea immediately grabbed the hand, lifted the body it was attached to (which, of course, was the Chawmnu), and bashed it against a big rock. The Chawmnu's head split open and her brains splattered. A bit of the splattered brains fell on Tlumtea's eyes, and he began to be able to see. When he realized that this was a cure for blindness, he took another lump of brains and spread it all over his eyes. Soon he had fully regained his vision. He did the same for his brothers, and all of them were able to see once more.

Once they regained their vision, they started farming on jhum land, where they sometimes stayed overnight, weeding the fields. This jhum field was in a place where it was common to find evil spirits and demons. They took turns cooking their meals in the little shack on their jhum field. Kaptheia, the oldest, was the first to stay back and cook the meal for his brothers.

As soon as he started cooking, another Chawmnu came and asked, "Kapthei, which will you give me; your life or your food?" Kaptheia replied, "My life over food, of course," and gave her all his cooked food. When his brothers came back, they had to wait for a fresh batch of food to finish cooking. This kept happening for each of the brothers when it was their turn to cook. After a hard day's work, the brothers would always have to wait hungrily for a fresh batch of food to be cooked before they could have their evening meal. Tlumtea got very annoyed at this state of affairs, but his brothers told him, "You'll see when your turn comes."

Finally it was Tlumtea's turn to cook the evening meal for his brothers. As he waited for the food to cook, he wove a large basket with a lid. As usual, the Chawmnu came, and as usual she asked, "Which will you give me, your life or your food?"

Tlumtea replied, "I would rather give you food than my life." The Chawmnu confidently reached for the food, but Tlumtea said, "It is not yet cooked, why don't you take a seat and wait?"

So the Chawmnu sat and waited near the basket Tlumtea had woven. "What is this basket for?" she asked.

Tlumtea replied, "It is to carry a huge rooster that we own. It must be about your size. If you can fit in the basket, it should be big enough for the rooster. Why don't you test it?"

As soon as the Chawmnu got into the basket, Tlumtea closed the lid and secured it. Then he said, "I will keep you caged in this basket and children will poke at you and use you for entertainment."

The Chawmnu became very afraid and said, "Tlumte, let me redeem myself."

"How?" asked Tlumtea, and the Chawmnu replied, "I will trade my freedom for knives, for all of you; axes for all of you, spears for all of you, shovels for all of you, bison for all of you, and finally, a wife for each one of you."

Tlumtea said, "Very well then. Give all of them to me now." And by the Chawmnu's magic, everything that she had promised him appeared before them—all except the bison. "Those I will give to you later," she said.

The brothers settled down with their wives. After some months had passed, they decided it was time they left their house to bring the bison that had been promised to them. The bison were in a far-off place, and the Chawmnu had given them directions. It is said that they were never heard from again.

While they were gone, the Chawmnu came to their wives whom they had left behind. "I am thirsty, can you give me some water?" she said. The wife of the oldest brother gave her some water, and the Chawmnu promptly gobbled her up. She then went back to the house to ask for more water, and every time they gave her water, she ate up the person who brought it to her.

She spared only Tlumtea's pregnant wife, who was in labor. As all of this was happening, she had given birth to a son. Weakly, she, too, managed to give some water to the Chawmnu. As soon as she did so, the Chawmnu took hold of her hand and dragged her along and brought her home to live with her. Meanwhile, the abandoned son she had just given birth to somehow survived on his own.

As the child grew up, he made up his mind to look for his mother. Looking for things around the house that he could bring along on his adventure, he found some money that had been left behind a long time ago by his father and uncles.

On his way to find his mother, one day he arrived at a village. The villagers asked him, "Fahrahte, where are you going?" He replied, "You call me an orphan?!" (For that is what Fahrahtea means). "I am looking for somebody who can turn me into a mouse." The chief of the village said, "I can do it." Fahrahtea paid the chief the money he had brought along with him, and in exchange, the chief said, "Turn into a mouse!" and he turned into a mouse.

Fahrahtea sneakily espied where the chief stored the money that he had given him, which was at the bottom of a woven basket, and that night, while everybody was asleep, he climbed into the basket and stole back the money.

The next day, having turned himself back into human form, he went to another village, and headed for the chief's house. There, the chief asked him, "Fahrahte, where are you going?" And he replied, "You call me an orphan?! I am looking for someone who can turn me into a carpenter bee." He struck the same deal with the chief of this new village, who turned him into a carpenter bee. And just as before, he stole the money back from the chief's hiding place that night.

The next day, he went to yet another village, where he met the chief, and had a similar encounter. He said, "I am looking for someone who could turn me into a chubby, lovable toddler." The chief did as the other chiefs had done and turned him into a chubby, lovable child. That night, Fahrahtea turned himself into mouse, and stole back the money again. He could now turn himself into a mouse, a bee, or a toddler whenever he wished.

When daybreak came, he turned himself into a carpenter bee and flew away towards the Chawmnu's village where his mother lived. Once he reached there, he turned into his normal human form and introduced himself to his mother. They had a joyful reunion.

He said to his mother, "Mother, later, you must say to the Chawmnu, 'Let us reveal to each other who our creators are,' and if she says, 'You go first,' you must tell her a lie. You must say, 'the ones who created me are the fish in the river.' "

After this, his mother hid him so that the Chawmnu would not see him.

Later, the Chawmnu came home. His mother said, "Chawmnu, we have stayed together in this house for a long time. Let us tell each other who our creators are."

The Chawmnu replied, "You tell me first."

Fahrahtea's mother said, "The ones who created me are the fish in the river. What about you?"

The Chawmnu said, "The one who created me is the pigeon with red wings."

The next morning, the Chawmnu went to the river to torture the fish. She showed them no mercy, but when she was done torturing them, she threw them back into the water. Meanwhile, Fahrahtea had turned himself into a bee, and witnessed everything. He flew back hurriedly to his mother and told her what the Chawmnu had done. He said to her, "When the Chawmnu returns, you must say, 'I don't know what is wrong with me today. I feel terribly sore, as if somebody had given me a beating.'"

When the Chawmnu returned in the evening, his mother said exactly what he had told her to say. This convinced the Chawmnu that the fish were indeed her creators. It made her satisfied to know that she could do whatever she wanted to her life source.

The next day, Fahrahtea set out to harm the Chawmnu's creator, the pigeon with the red wings, just as she herself had done to the fish. He turned himself into a bee and flew high into the air, toward the village in the sky. There he went to the chief's house and turned himself into a toddler. This chief was the guardian of the pigeon with red wings. This was the same bird that was the creator and life source of the Chawmnu.

When the chief saw the adorable child, he asked, "Whose child is this? Everybody must come and have a look." Everybody came to look, but no one could say that the child belonged to them. So, the chief said, "If this boy does not belong to anybody, he shall be mine," and took him as his own.

After a while, Fahrahtea, still in the guise of a child, said to his adoptive mother, "Mother, I want to play with the chickens." So they let him play with their chickens. But soon, he pretended he was tired of playing with them.

The next morning, he said, "Mother, I want to play with the eggs." And so they let him. But soon he acted bored again and returned the eggs.

Finally, he said, "Mother, I want to play with the red-winged pigeon." But his mother protested, "You cannot play with that, for it is my creator and my source of life, and you might harm it." But Fahrahtea promised he would not harm the bird and so, they let him play with it.

The next day came, and once more, he asked to play with the red-winged pigeon. They allowed him to do so, because they trusted that he would not harm it. But as soon as they gave him the bird, he flew with it back to his real mother's house.

Once back at his mother's house, the Chawmnu was livid to see that Fahrahtea had possession of the red-winged pigeon, and a fight ensued. Fahrahtea's mother leapt to her son's defense and fought with the evil being. At one point, Fahrahtea's mother cried out, "Son, I am not able to defeat her. Break one of the bird's wings!" He did so, but his mother still could not overpower the Chawmnu. "I am still not able to overpower her, break the other wing!" she cried. He did so, but his mother still could not defeat the Chawmnu, so she told him, "Break one of the bird's knees!" and when that did not help, he broke the other knee as well. However, the Chawmnu was not ready to admit defeat, and she continued to attack Fahrahtea's mother by butting her with her head. His mother desperately shouted, "I still cannot defeat her! You had better break the bird's neck!" and so he did. The Chawmnu finally died. And so, mother and son were finally able to live a peaceful and happy life together.

The Story of Vanchung Nula

Once upon a time, there was a maiden. Everyone called her Vanchung Nula or Sky Maiden. Nobody knew her real name, but her beauty was known all over the land. She was so beautiful that all the bachelors wanted to marry her; they vied for her attention, but none could win her over.

Meanwhile, there was a group of brothers who were all bachelors who lived in the land. The youngest of the lot was called Tlumtea. These brothers, like everyone else, had also heard of the beautiful Vanchung Nula and so they made up their minds to woo her as well. Decked in their finest clothes and grandest accoutrements, they set out towards the place where she lived.

As they made their way, they were proud of the way they looked, handsome and dressed in all their glory. Tlumtea, the youngest, led the way, and behind him all his brothers followed.

Soon, they met a passerby, and asked him, "We are headed off to woo the beautiful Sky Maiden; who among us looks the most handsome?"

The passerby said, "The one in front. Tlumtea."

This displeased his brothers, and so they made him walk in the middle. As they went further on, after a while, they met some more passersby and asked them the same question. They were met with the same reply: "Tlumtea."

As people kept favoring Tlumtea, his brothers became even more jealous, and made him walk at the very end of the procession.

After some time, they reached a village where they met many villagers on the street. The brothers paused to speak to them and said, "We are on our way to woo Vanchung Nula. Which one of us looks the finest?" The villagers replied, "The one at the very back. Tlumtea." This was the last straw for his brothers. They became inflamed with jealousy and sent him home.

The rest of the brothers proceeded on towards Vanchung Nula's house in the sky, and finally reached it. Full of confidence, they sauntered into her house where she received them gracefully and rushed to provide them with stools to sit on. Once they were seated, she went to her father and told him, "Father, we have guests."

Her father replied, "Are they good guests or bad guests?"

Vanchung Nula replied, "Bad ones."

Her father then curtly said, "Give them porridge made of grain husks and send them home."

So, she gave them the porridge and sent them on their way home.

Shortly afterwards, Tlumtea, who had been denied the opportunity before, decided to go on his own and try his luck with Vanchung Nula. As he walked along, he saw a bird being circled by an eagle who was on the verge of catching it. Tlumtea felt sorry for the bird and chased the eagle away. The bird flew off happily.

After undertaking the journey to Vanchung Nula's house, he finally reached it. When Vanchung Nula saw Tlumtea, she was besotted with how handsome he was and gave him very special attention. She even told him secrets that she had never told any of her other suitors. These secrets were the correct answers to any question he might be asked later to prove his worth.

Vanchung Nula, as she always did, went to her father and told him, "Father, come, we have a guest."

Her father asked, "A good guest or a bad one?"

Vanchung Nula replied, "A good guest."

Her father said, "Well then, give him rice and meat wrapped in leaves and send him on his way." She gave him the food as her father bade her, and her father left them to go and work in the fields.

However, because she was so enraptured by Tlumtea's charms, she did not want to send him away. In the evening, when her father came home, he saw that Tlumtea was still there and that his daughter was completely taken by him. When he realized that Tlumtea, too, desired to marry his daughter, he began to ask him some questions.

His first question was, "If you really mean to marry my daughter, which direction does our floor face?"

Vanchung Nula, of course, had already revealed the correct responses to Tlumtea, so he confidently replied, "The west," and it was the right reply.

Her father then asked his next question, "Alright then, which way does our house pillar face?"

Tlumtea easily replied, "Towards the floor," and it was correct again.

Vanchung Nula's father had one more task for Tlumtea. "If you really want to marry my daughter, take this spoon and fetch water from the well with it. But you must not wet the bottom of the spoon. If you can do that, you may marry my daughter," he said.

Unfortunately, Vanchung Nula had not told Tlumtea how to fetch water with a spoon without wetting its bottom. Tlumtea silently panicked. He walked towards the well, wondering how he would accomplish the task before him. As he worried about his task, he happened to remember the bird that he had saved on his way to the Sky Maiden's house. Desperately, he called for the bird, hoping that it would somehow be able to help him.

The little bird heard Tlumtea calling it and hastily flew towards his voice. It perched on a tree branch near where Tlumtea stood. Tlumtea told the bird all about the difficult task set before him and how he needed help. The little bird said, "Don't worry. I know what to do." So saying, it flew into the well, filled its mouth with as much water as it could hold, flew back out, and spit it out into the spoon. The little bird kept doing this until the spoon was filled to the brim, and the bottom of the spoon never got wet. Tlumtea showed this to Vanchung Nula's father. Having accomplished the task set before him, Vanchung Nula's father had no more objections, and so Tlumtea won the hand of the lovely maiden. They were soon happily married.

Now, Vanchung Nula's abode was in the sky, but Tlumtea lived on the land below. Since they were now married, it was necessary for Tlumtea to bring his new bride to his home. As they made the journey to his house, she became thirsty. While Tlumtea went to fetch water for her, he asked her to wait on the top of the hogplum tree.

Soon a Taunu came hobbling by. (A Taunu is a nasty female evil spirit that lives in dark forests and looks and acts very much like a Phungpuinu. In fact, some say it may be just another name for a Phungpuinu; and if you have read the story earlier in the book about the Phungpuinu, you will recognize a lot of what happens next, because the Taunu says and does almost all the same things that the Phungpuinu does in that story. But not quite.)

The Taunu squatted next to the hogplum tree. She peeled off her scalp, held it in front of her, and proceeded to search through her hair for lice, popping the little insects whenever she found them.

After some time had passed, the Taunu happened to see the shadow of Vanchung Nula on the ground in front of her. She could see that the shadow was adorned with bangles and many necklaces, and the Taunu thought it was her own shadow. She found herself very beautiful, and proudly chanted, much like a Phungpuinu had sung when she saw Tumchhingi's shadow:

"Though my body be plain and bare
My shadow is adorned with pretty bangles
and many dangling necklaces!"

and she hopped around with glee.

When Vanchung Nula heard the commotion below, she peered down from the top of the hogplum tree, and was very amused. She shouted, "Haha! That's my shadow, not yours."

The Taunu looked up, saw her, and was irked. She said, "The insolence! But you're right. It is indeed your shadow. Come down immediately or else!"

Hearing the threat, Vanchung Nula scurried down the tree, but once she reached the ground, the Taunu swallowed her whole! However, Vanchung Nula did not stay inside the Taunu, but promptly exited from her bottom in the form of a long, sturdy gourd-stem.

When Tlumtea returned with the water he had gone to fetch, he found only the Taunu. He exclaimed, "You do not look like my Vanchung Nula! Even your hands have turned long and pointy."

"Someone asked me where you went. I answered, 'Tlumtea has gone that way,' and pointed in that direction. So my fingers became long and pointy," was the Taunu's reply.

"And why have your eyes turned so goopy and gooey?" asked Tlumtea next.

"They have turned goopy and gooey from watching and waiting for you to come back to me."

Tlumtea, having no choice but to believe her, dejectedly walked behind the Taunu, wondering how she could have changed so much while she was gone. When they neared the village, they saw that all the villagers had excitedly gathered at the village entrance to welcome Tlumtea and his beautiful new bride, the famed Vanchung Nula. But when they saw the Taunu, they all exclaimed in surprise, "How ugly she is!" and Tlumtea was very embarrassed.

When they reached Tlumtea's house, the Taunu acted like a normal human and they got ready to start their new life as man and wife. Tlumtea still had the gourd stem with him; he had seen it on the ground back when he had first encountered the Taunu, and had brought it home because it was such a beautiful stem. Now, he put it safely on the shelf above the cooking fire. As life went on, Tlumtea and the Taunu went every day to their field to work, and while they were gone, the gourd stem would turn itself back into Vanchung Nula. She would then cook their meals for them while they were gone. This astounded Tlumtea (just as Raldawna had been baffled by Tumchhingi's mysterious cooking) because there was always food already prepared for them whenever they came home.

One day, Tlumtea told the Taunu to go ahead without him and he hid himself in the house, determined to catch whoever had been preparing their meals for them. He bundled himself in the big family quilt and waited patiently. When it was time to cook the evening meal, Vanchung Nula hopped down from her perch on the shelf. Tlumtea peered from his hiding place and was surprised to see that it was indeed his beloved Vanchung Nula. He made up his mind to try and catch her. As she prepared the fire for cooking, Tlumtea stealthily pounced on her from behind. Vanchung Nula cried out, "Let me go Tlumte, let me go! I am terrified of your wife." She then told him everything that had happened including how she had been swallowed by the Taunu and how she had become a gourd stem.

Tlumtea said, "Do not fear anymore. I shall kill the Taunu."

And so, they were reunited and spent the afternoon together, talking and laughing happily. When the Taunu came home from her day's work in the field, she could hear the lighthearted giggles from inside the house. She called out angrily, "Tlumte, open the door for me. Who is it that you are cavorting with on my marital bed while I have been gone?"

Tlumtea ignored her and would not open the door. The incensed Taunu bore the door down with her body and tumbled into the house. She ground her teeth in anger when she saw Vanchung Nula inside.

Tlumtea then decided, "The two of you must fight; whoever wins shall be my wife."

For their weapons, he gave the Taunu a sword made of Khawmhma, the sumac plant, and for her shield, a husk from the plantain tree. To Vanchung Nula, he gave a sharp, long knife, and for a shield he gave her a piece of sturdy cloth; then he made them face each other for combat.

Vanchung Nula said, "You may strike me first," so the Taunu struck a hard blow at her, but it made no impact since her weapon was a flimsy plant. Vanchung Nula then struck back and beheaded the Taunu with one swift blow. They dumped the Taunu's body in the garden where it grew into a Saisu plant. From then on, Tlumtea and Vanchung Nula lived happily ever after.

The Story of Chawngmawii & Hrangchhuana

Once upon a time, there were two villages at war with each other. In one of the villages there lived a very beautiful girl named Chawngmawii, and in the other village there lived a very handsome young man named Hrangchhuana, who was her secret lover. Both of them were well-known and popular in their respective villages on account of their good looks.

But because of the animosity between Hrangchhuana's village and Chawngmawii's village, they could not meet each other openly. Hrangchhuana had to sneak into Chawngmawii's village at night to meet her. He did this so often that he became quite bold about it. He grew so audacious that after visiting Chawngmawii at night, he would abduct a small child and carry it back to his own village.

When the children started to go missing, the people of Chawngmawii's village were of course very upset. They set to work building a tall fence all the way around the village. At the gate, they sprinkled ashes on the ground, so as to catch the footprints of the kidnapper.

But Hrangchhuana was very clever. He kept right on sneaking into the village at night when the guards weren't looking, but he would walk in backwards through the gate, so that his footprints made it look as if he were leaving. When the guards noticed the footprints, they would rush to search the surrounding forest, while Hrangchhuana was really inside. When he left, too, he would walk out backwards, so his footprints made it look as if he were coming in. Then the guards would make a frantic search of the village, when in fact Hrangchhuana was already gone.

Eventually, though, Hrangchhuana became careless, or perhaps his luck just ran out, and he was nabbed by the guards at the gate.

The chief of Chawngmawii's village was terribly angry, and he gave the order that Hrangchhuana be tied with rope and laid on the road in the middle of the village. Then the chief ordered all the women of the village to come out and walk over Hrangchhuana's prone body, placing one leg on either side of him, to humiliate him. Some of the women even urinated on his face. Finally it was Chawngmawii's turn. But instead of walking over him, she knelt down, covered Hrangchhuana's face with her shawl and held him tenderly, crying, "Oh, my dearest, what have they done to you?"

Thus Chawngmawii gave herself away as Hrangchhuana's secret lover. The people of the village were furious with her. As punishment, they tied her up and made her watch as Hrangchhuana was tortured. Finally they beheaded him, and hung his severed head on top of a tree near the village gate for all to see. People threw mud at his face and shouted insults. Poor Chawngmawii looked on with great sadness. At last she could no longer bear to see the head of her beloved being abused, and she took some water and climbed up the tree and washed Hrangchhuana's face clean.

Before his death, Hrangchhuana had told Chawngmawii, "If I am ever captured and put to death, you must take my head and give it to my parents. When they ask you if you will accept something as a reward, ask for the ball of thread that I have kept in the basket."

So Chawngmawii began to look for a chance to steal Hrangchhuana's head. One night when everyone was asleep, she finally got the chance she had been waiting for. She climbed the tree, removed Hrangchhuana's head, and set off towards his village.

When she reached Hrangchhuana's house, she stood outside the door and sang:

"Open to me, O parents of Chhuana,
The head of my beloved
I bring to your door."

Hrangchhuana's parents were heartbroken to see their son's lifeless face, but they greatly appreciated Chawngmawii's gesture of returning the head to them. They told her they would give her anything she wanted that they could afford to give. Chawngmawii sang:

"I don't want any great reward,
Just a tiny thing;
Give me the ball of thread
That is in your basket stored."

Hrangchhuana's parents were very surprised by this request, but nevertheless they gave Chawngmawii the ball of thread. What they didn't know was that concealed within the ball of thread was a very valuable necklace pendant. Chawngmawii kept this pendant, and wore it happily in remembrance of her lover.

But even this happiness was short-lived, for when the people of her village discovered that she had stolen Hrangchhuana's head and given it to the parents, they decided that Chawngmawii must be put to death. And so they killed her.

Though their lives were short, the spirit of their love survives today in the starry sky. Chawngmawii is the Mizo name for the planet Venus, and Hrangchhuana is the name for the planet Jupiter. Every once in a rare while, these two planets approach each other in the sky, and sometimes they come together in what is known today as a planetary conjunction. At such times, the souls of Hrangchhuana and Chawngmawii unite, and they make love.

It is said that if young lovers make a date for the night when the two planets are together in the sky, they are sure to get lucky!

About the Author

Cherrie Lalnunziri Chhangte taught literature at Mizoram University, India for 18 years before she took an early retirement to focus on her family and her writing. She earned a Ph.D. in African American literature under the Department of English at Northeastern Hill University (NEHU) and was a recipient of a Fulbright post-doctoral fellowship at Stanford University, California, where she worked on folk narratives of Native American and Indian tribals. As she was already an avid scholar of folk studies, this furthered her interest in folktales and prompted her to translate Mizo folk narratives for a wider audience. She now lives in Chicago, USA, with her husband and two daughters, where she spends her time writing and going on long, meandering walks in between mommy duties.